"Hey, sweetheart, what'd I tell you!" The words, spoken from behind her, made Betsy wince. Trouble, she knew, was approaching in the person of Dudley deShon . . .

"Your dad agreed with me that you need some time to have fun, and that I'm the guy to help you have it."

Pete's eyebrows had drawn together and his face was slowly turning red. He said, "Betsy, I thought you had to—"

As if Dudley had just noticed Pete, he said, "Oh, hi. I'm afraid you'll have to excuse my girl right now, young man. Betsy and I have plans for the rest of the day." Betsy saw a flash of anger in Pete's gray eyes.

"I'm Dudley deShon." He offered his hand. "What'll I call you?"

Pete did not shake hands. Instead he glared directly at Dudley and said, his mouth twisting into a sneer, "Just call me a sucker!"

Caprice Romances from Tempo Books

DANCE WITH A STRANGER by *Elizabeth Van Steenwyk*
BEFORE LOVE by *Gloria D. Miklowitz*
SUNRISE by *G. C. Wisler*
THREE'S A CROWD by *Nola Carlson*
A SPECIAL LOVE by *Harriette S. Abels*
SOMEONE FOR SARA by *Judith Enderle*
S.W.A.K. SEALED WITH A KISS by *Judith Enderle*
COLOR IT LOVE by *Amy Lawrence*
CARRIE LOVES SUPERMAN by *Gloria D. Miklowitz*
PROGRAMMED FOR LOVE by *Judith Enderle*
A NEW LOVE FOR LISA by *Harriette S. Abels*
WISH FOR TOMORROW by *Pam Ketter*
THE BOY NEXT DOOR by *Wendy Storm*
A HAT FULL OF LOVE by *Barbara Steiner*
TWO LOVES FOR TINA by *Maurine Miller*
LOVE IN FOCUS by *Margaret Meacham*
DO YOU REALLY LOVE ME? by *Jeanne R. Lenz*
A BICYCLE BUILT FOR TWO by *Susan Shaw*
A NEW FACE IN THE MIRROR by *Nola Carlson*
TOO YOUNG TO KNOW by *Margaret M. Scariano*
SURFER GIRL by *Francess Lin Lantz*
LOVE BYTE by *Helane Zeiger*
WHEN WISHES COME TRUE by *Judith Enderle*
HEARTBREAKER by *Terry Hunter*
LOVE NOTES by *Leah Dionne*
NEVER SAY NEVER by *Ann Boyle*

A CAPRICE ROMANCE

Never Say Never

Ann Boyle

TEMPO BOOKS, NEW YORK

NEVER SAY NEVER

A Tempo Book/published by arrangement with
the author

PRINTING HISTORY
Tempo Original/January 1984
Second printing/July 1984

All rights reserved.
Copyright © 1984 by Ann Boyle
This book may not be reproduced in whole or in part,
by mimeograph or any other means, without permission.
For information address: The Berkley Publishing Group,
200 Madison Avenue, New York, N.Y. 10016

ISBN: 0-441-56972-2

"Caprice" and the stylized Caprice logo are trademarks
belonging to The Berkley Publishing Group.

Tempo Books are published by The Berkley Publishing Group,
200 Madison Avenue, New York, New York 10016.
Tempo Books are registered in the United States Patent Office.
PRINTED IN THE UNITED STATES OF AMERICA

Chapter One

A light shower of fine sand, blown on the desert wind, made Betsy Alexander close her eyes and duck her head as she walked along the sidewalk that led to Desertview High School. Even with her eyes closed she could feel that she was the object of someone's scrutiny, and the feeling was not pleasant. As soon as the gust of wind had passed Betsy opened her eyes and met the hostile stares of three girls who stood in the shelter of the roof's overhang.

For a few seconds the three pairs of eyes locked on Betsy. Then the girls turned toward each other, exchanged smirks, and, linking arms, moved toward the door of the building. Before they went through the doorway Betsy heard one of them say, clearly and distinctly, so as to be overheard, "She's the one that's moved into the dump."

It is not a dump! Betsy didn't know for sure whether she had shouted the words aloud or only thought them, but the girls moved on and the door swung shut behind them, closing Betsy out as if they had shut her out of their lives.

A red haze of anger filled Betsy's vision so that she walked blindly, clenching her fists until her nails dug into her palms. She reached the door and somehow managed to wrench it open. Determined not to show the inner turmoil that was tearing her apart, she kept on walking toward another door over which hung a sign, OFFICE. After all, these three girls didn't represent the entire school. Desertview High might be a small school, but there must be people here that were more friendly than these girls, people who knew that the Sagebrush Recreational Vehicle Campground wasn't a dump.

It hadn't been easy for Betsy to come alone this morning to enroll in a new school after the fall term had begun. Nothing had been easy since her mother's last bout of pneumonia when the doctors back in Chicago had warned her that living in a drier climate was imperative if she hoped to regain her health.

Betsy had hated leaving the only home she could remember. She had hated leaving her friends, her school, everything familiar, to move to Shelter Valley, a small desert community in Southern California.

"You're going to live in a trailer camp!" her close friend Cindy Thomas cried when she heard the news. "Oh, you poor thing."

"Don't call it a trailer camp!" Betsy said. "It's a recreational vehicle park that Daddy's buying, and he says there's a real house on the grounds and we'll live in that." Although Betsy was as totally horrified as Cindy sounded, the last thing she wanted was to have Cindy feel sorry for her. That wouldn't make things easier. It wouldn't make her like the desert either. I'll never like it, she thought.

She hadn't even told her parents how she hated the desert. They didn't need a complaining daughter to add to their worries. Her father had sold his small furniture store and put the money into the RV campground. "Camping is a big thing in the West," he said. "In the desert it can be an all-year recreation, and with the three of us working around the place, we should make a go of it." He had sounded so enthusiastic that although Betsy guessed he hated giving up his life in

Chicago as much as she did, she knew she could do no less than her share of adjusting.

But everything here was so different. Everything was weird, like the landscape that was all brown, sandy earth cluttered with rocks and stones and stubby cactus. Now and then one of those weird growths called Joshua trees that weren't really trees at all popped up out of the barrenness. But they only made the scene more grotesque with their shaggy, angular limbs raised like a scarecrow's arms.

Only her father had seen the campground or even the town of Shelter Valley before they moved. Mr. Alexander hadn't told them about the old ruin that filled one corner of the property with an unsightly clutter, and seeing it for the first time was a shock to Betsy, and probably to her mother. But her dad's enthusiasm had not wavered. "As soon as we get the campground in shape," he said, "we'll make short work of clearing away that mess. Betsy can help after school and on weekends, and you, Sharon, can do what you feel up to." He had put his arm around Betsy's mother and kissed her as he said, "Already your color is better, darling."

Seeing their love and faith in each other sent a wave of loneliness sweeping over Betsy. They had each other to give support when things got bad, but she had no one to cheer her up when she was down.

In the next instant Betsy scolded herself for moping around. Her parents loved her. She never doubted that. But there were some things you just couldn't admit to your parents. Like how the three girls really got to her with their slimy remark.

They had probably been trying to test her, she told herself, to see if she could take it and what she would do. What she really wanted to do was to rush after them and punch each one in the nose. Hard!

But getting into a fight was more like the way a fourth-grader would act. A fifteen-year-old should be more mature. Besides, getting into a fight could land her in trouble with the school as well as with her parents, and even theirs. Above all, it was no way to start off in a new school, in a new community, when she wanted to help her mother get her health back. Betsy kept digging her fingernails into her palms until the pain distracted her thoughts and eventually managed to clear her vision.

By the time she reached the office she had regained some of her self-control, although she felt that her face must still be flushed. She tried to relax her facial muscles into a pleasant expression as she opened the door and stepped inside.

There was only one desk in the outer office where she stood, and behind it sat a woman who appeared to be a little younger than Betsy's mother. She was typing, the clack, clack of the keys of the manual machine making a jarring note. Somehow that helped to restore Betsy to relative calmness, possibly because it gave her something different to think about. The woman continued to concentrate on her work, apparently unaware of Betsy's presence. For a few seconds Betsy watched her in silence. Dark hair framed her oval face in soft curls, and although her eyes were downcast, intent on her work so that Betsy could not see their expression, her mouth appeared to be relaxed in a pleasant half-smile.

Betsy grew uncomfortable as she continued to stand waiting for the woman to notice her. Perhaps she hadn't heard the door open. The typewriter's clacking was loud enough to cover a sharper sound than that. Betsy cleared her throat.

The woman looked up quickly and smiled. "Oh," she said. "I hope I haven't kept you waiting long. I didn't hear you come in." The smile widened into a grin. "This machine makes enough noise to wake King Tut in his tomb, but I'm just grateful that it works. We don't have much money in our school fund and I'd hate to go back to writing everything by hand. Now, what can I do for you?"

"I came to enroll. I'm transferring to Desertview."

"Oh, of course." She reached into a drawer and pulled out a form sheet. "You're the people who bought the—"

Betsy couldn't let another person say it to her. Before the woman could complete her sentence, and before Betsy could stop herself, she leaned forward across the desk and blurted out, "It isn't a dump! It isn't!" Her own words horrified her and she clapped her hand over her mouth and whispered, "I shouldn't have said that."

The woman's eyes were understanding. "You have a right to defend your new home. But let me explain that I wasn't about to say what you thought. I know that it isn't a dump. You are fortunate to live in a spot that's rich in history. The Butterfield Stagecoach once ran along the line of your property, and there's a wealth of history in your own yard, no matter how many of the kids chop it down."

Betsy looked at her. Did this woman guess that those girls had given her a bad time? It was nice of her to try to make me feel better, Betsy thought. But who in Shelter Valley cared about a stagecoach that had long ago gone out of existence? For that matter, how could the Alexander family take time to care when they had so many more immediate problems on their hands? Like the run-down state of the Sagebrush RV Campground, for instance. The mesquite and creosote bush had just about taken over the campsites, and the heavy rains had washed gullies throughout the area. Not even that load of gravel and the hard work she and her father had put in all last weekend had done much to improve its appearance. Who was this woman that she could say Betsy was fortunate to live in Sagebrush RV Park?

As if in answer to her thoughts, the woman said, "By the way, I'm Mrs. Nesbit. I double in brass as the office secretary in between teaching a couple of classes. Right now let's get you set up in a schedule."

For a while they discussed classes and schedules, and then Mrs. Nesbit handed Betsy a form to fill out, waving her to a chair with a wide arm that stood with others against the wall of the room. "Sit down and fill that out," she said. "Then you can go right to your homeroom and get there when the others do."

Betsy discovered that in Desertview High her choice of subjects was more limited than it had been in Chicago. But her first judgment of Mrs. Nesbit as a likable person held firm. She hoped she would have her for at least one class.

Mrs. Nesbit went back to her typing, and Betsy tackled the form she was to fill out. While she was debating between the limited choice of art or home ec, the door opened again and a boy about her own age came into the room. "Hi, Mrs. N." He grinned as he held out a thick folder. "Here's Mr. Brock's report you wanted. But he said you rushed him so he didn't have time to get it in shape. He said I was to wait and see if you could read it, then bring back any pages you couldn't and he'd do them over."

"Not again! Thanks to that man, I'll be totally gray before the year is out." She shook her head as if in despair, but her smile was indulgent. It was clear that she didn't really dislike the apparently disorganized Mr. Brock.

"Hang in there, Mrs. N.," the boy said. "You'll make the scene okay."

"Thanks, Pete," Mrs. Nesbit said. "I can always count on your support."

He hadn't noticed Betsy. At least he gave no sign that he had. She drew her arms closer to her sides and tried to become invisible, hoping he wouldn't notice her. She couldn't take another reminder that she lived in a dump.

"Anything I can do for you before I go to my homeroom, Mrs. N.?" Pete asked. "I have a few minutes before the bell rings."

"As a matter of fact, there is something, Pete,"

Mrs. Nesbit said with a sweep of her hand that directed the boy's gray eyes toward Betsy. "Betsy, this is Pete Davis who knows his way around Desertview High."

Betsy said a quick "hi," and received his wide grin in reply as Mrs. Nesbit said to him, "Betsy's transferring to Desertview. She and her family have just moved to Shelter Valley. As soon as she has filled out her enrollment form, would you show her where her homeroom is?"

She had switched from the introduction to her request so quickly that Betsy was sure it was done to keep Pete from making some remark about her living in the dump. "I can find it myself," she said, rushing the words. "I'm sure I can."

"Don't turn down a good opportunity, Betsy," Mrs. Nesbit said. "Pete is one of my favorite young guys. Dependable enough even for me."

Pete gave a rueful shrug and raised his eyebrows. "You sure don't make me sound very exciting, Mrs. N."

"Pete, there are any number of qualities that are more important than being exciting."

"Yeah? Well, I wish you'd convince Stacy of that."

"Stacy's well aware of your good qualities, Pete," Mrs. Nesbit said. But Betsy noticed that she glanced away from Pete as she said that, and although she chuckled, her lips had a stiffness that might have meant disapproval. Then with her usual easy warmth, she said, "Now run along, kids, before I have to write out a hall pass for you. That second bell will ring any minute. And I've got to get to work on Mr. Brock's report."

"Sure you can decipher all the pages?" Pete asked.

"Pete, I've been deciphering Ralph Brock's handwriting for years now. I'm sure I can do another sheaf of pages. But thanks anyway for your offer." She walked with them to the door and with a smile waved them on their way.

Pete was just about Betsy's height, she noticed as

she walked beside him along the corridor, but his legs must have been longer because she had trouble keeping up with his stride. Or maybe it was because she was breathless from trying to think of something to say to him.

They walked in silence for a time, but at last he said, "You a junior?"

"No. A sophomore." As she said the word, it suddenly sounded totally juvenile. Only a few short months ago being promoted from freshman to sophomore had seemed a miracle of success, but now she felt all awkward adolescent, with her tongue and her mind frozen into silence in the presence of this boy who was undoubtedly older. Not only did he think she lived in a dump, but he probably thought of her as a mere child. As she walked beside Pete Davis, close enough to touch, Betsy felt as cut off from him as if a concrete and steel wall separated them.

The corridor was filling up with students now, and it seemed to Betsy that almost everyone they passed had a friendly greeting for Pete. Mrs. Nesbit must have thought being seen with such a popular boy would do her some good with the other kids here. Now she'd better think of something to say to him or he'd spread a bad word about her. "Are you a junior, or a senior?" she asked.

"Me?" Pete turned to grin at her. "I'm a sophomore, just like you."

Betsy was so surprised she couldn't say anything.

There was another long silence, an uncomfortable one for Betsy as she tried to think what her friend Cindy would say. But nothing would come to her mind.

At last Pete broke the silence. "You ever lived in the desert before?"

"No. I'd never even seen the desert until we came here to live."

"Really! Well, what do you think of the desert?"

"It's—it's different."

"Ye-ah." He drew the word out. "Isn't it great?"

"Great?" Was he serious? A quick glance at him showed her he was, very much so. "Well, I . . . I really don't know enough about it . . . That is, I haven't seen much except . . . I don't know what I think of it yet."

"You'll get to know the desert. Then you'll be turned on the way I am. Don't go wandering around on your own in the desert, you know, off the roads and away from civilization, until you know something about it."

The very thought of going out into the desert made Betsy shudder. "Why should I wander around in the desert?" she asked. "Why would anyone want to do that?"

He turned to look at her as if he couldn't believe he had heard her correctly. "Because it's so great out there." His eyes seemed to have filmed over as if he were seeing beyond the walls of the school building, looking out over that vast emptiness.

Pete's hair was light, bleached by the sun, and a sprinkling of freckles spattered his cheekbones. He grinned and turned to her. "There's so much to see out there," he said. "So much to do."

Betsy knew there was lots to do, all right, but it wasn't the kind of thing she could really get excited about doing, like clearing brush and windblown litter away from the campsites as she helped her father get the campground ready for the campers. Then there was that unsightly pile of rubble that made people call the campground a dump. Her father had said it was the ruin of an old adobe building, and Mrs. Nesbit called it history, but the high school kids thought of it as a dump. Betsy felt that she had been branded by coming to live there. She could really sympathize with that poor woman in Nathaniel Hawthorne's story, the one who had a scarlet letter sewn on her dress.

"Maybe I'll show you something about the desert one of these days," Pete said. "Okay?"

Betsy was so surprised she could only stare at him. Was he kidding? He didn't appear to be, and Betsy grinned at him. It might even be worth going out into the desolate desert if it meant having Pete Davis for a friend.

They had reached her homeroom, and he left her to go to his own.

For a moment Betsy stood in the doorway watching Pete Davis stride away down the hall. She was so absorbed that she didn't see the three girls approach, and as they brushed past her she was swept off balance so that she bumped into the pale blond one.

"Why don't you look where you're going?" the girl said, giving her a scornful look. The other two imitated her glance, and the chubby girl said, "Well, what can you expect from someone who lives at the dump?"

As the girls moved on into the room, the blond girl said, as if continuing a conversation interrupted by the unpleasant incident, "—and of course I'm taking Pete Davis."

"Naturally," the other two said in chorus.

The blond girl must be the Stacy that Pete had mentioned to Mrs. Nesbit. She must be his girl, and before long she would have him convinced that Betsy was trash because she lived in a dump.

It isn't a dump! her mind cried out again. But what was the use of denying it? These girls would never believe her any more than she would ever like the desert.

Betsy went into the room and found a vacant chair. As she sat down she thought, Will my life be this dismal from now on?

Chapter Two

When Betsy came home from school that first afternoon her mother was waiting to hear all about her first day at Desertview High. "Did you meet some nice young people?" Sharon Alexander asked.

Betsy drew in a long breath and sat down in the canvas chair beside her mother. The sunshine had brought more color to her mother's face than Betsy had seen there for a long time. She seemed more relaxed too. "I haven't had much time yet to socialize. The teachers kept us busy."

"I've always heard that small-town people are friendly. You'll probably have no trouble making friends here."

She was looking at Betsy, and Betsy chose her words carefully as she said with a laugh, "Well, at least I found out who runs the student body." She told her about the three girls, Stacy, Tina, and Margo. But she did not tell what they had said about her living in a dump. "Mr. Logan, my English teacher, calls them the triad. They're always together and they seem to think with one mind. They have the last word. If they approve of me, I'm in. If they don't . . ." Betsy used a shrug of her shoulders to complete her thought.

"Oh, I'm sure they'll approve of you, once they get to know you, dear," her mother said with a loving smile.

Betsy wasn't so sure. She wasn't even sure she wanted to be taken into their charmed circle, not if that meant going meekly along with everything the three girls said. And yet, what if she had no friends at all?

Mr. Alexander came to join them. He wore an old pair of chino trousers and a work shirt, and his brown hair, usually so well groomed, straggled out from under a disreputable-looking hat. His shirt was stained with perspiration and his face glistened with moisture.

"Whew!" he said as he flung himself down into a chair. "Who'd guess this is October?"

Mrs. Alexander smiled. "Isn't that sun marvelous?"

"I could use a little less of its heat while I'm pushing to get a couple of campsites ready for the tourists I hope will come swarming in." He leaned over and patted his wife's hand. "But for you, sweetheart, I welcome the sun. Already it's doing good things for you. Anyway, if we were back in Chicago I'd be raking leaves now. Not exactly my favorite pastime."

Mrs. Alexander smiled at him. "And soon you'd be shoveling snow." He shuddered, wincing, and they laughed together. Then Mrs. Alexander began to talk about her plans for the campground. "Already I'm getting ideas. I want to plant a cactus garden out by the gate."

They seemed so happy to be here in this dismal desert that Betsy couldn't take any more. She stood up. "You look as if you could use some lemonade. I'll go make some."

Her father grinned. "Now that's the kind of daughter a man can be grateful for."

Betsy kissed him on the forehead and hurried into the house.

As she squeezed lemons over a pitcher, she thought the situation out more carefully. Her parents were great, really, making the best of a bad set of circumstances. She couldn't do less than pretend to be as cheerful as they were. The tangy scent of the lemons filled her nostrils, and she remembered the groves of lemon trees they had driven through on their way to Shelter Valley. All those acres of rich green leaves. Why couldn't her parents have settled in a place like that instead of this desolate spot? But as she stirred ice cubes into the pitcher of lemonade and set the pitcher and three glasses on a tray to carry outside, she knew the answer. The dry climate had already improved her mother's health. Besides, her parents' cheerful attitude reminded Betsy that she would have to adjust. At least she couldn't speak out about hating the desert. Still, telling herself to shape up didn't mean she'd always have a perfect record. She had to let go sometimes.

When she rejoined her parents they were talking about the view from the patio. "I've been watching the changing shadow patterns against those far hills," Mrs. Alexander said. "It's as good a show in a few hours as the changing seasons back East. You can actually see the shadows creep across the desert floor."

Betsy set down her burden and said, "I guess I'd better go change so that I can get to work. I'll rake the gravel in the driveway that leads to those two campsites you're working on, Daddy."

"Hey, aren't you going to have some of your own lemonade? What's the matter, you put cactus thorns in it or something?" He was grinning, and Betsy made herself grin back, although the reason she had to get away was that she couldn't bear to hear them compare this arid spot with their lovely home in the pleasant Chicago suburb. "No thorns, I promise," she said. "I did a lot of tasting in the kitchen."

Next morning and the following mornings when Betsy dressed for school, she tried to guess what Stacy, Tina and Margo would wear. Although she hated caring what they thought of her, she needed to win some friends.

Physically, Stacy, Tina, and Margo were as different as three girls of the same age could be. Margo was a tall, angular girl with chestnut brown hair; Tina was a short and plump brunette, but it was Stacy who was the really beautiful one. Her ash blond hair made a startling contrast to the deep golden tan of her flawlessly smooth skin. If only I looked like that, Betsy thought as she bemoaned her easily burned complexion, I'd never have another worry.

The three girls defied the differences in their appearance by wearing their hair in identical long, straight sweeps parted in the center. They invariably dressed in similar outfits too. When one wore a sweater and skirt, all did. If their costume happened to be jeans, the same designer's name appeared on the rear pockets of all. They always looked well turned out, as if their blouses never wrinkled, the hems of their skirts never raveled, their nail polish never chipped.

Perhaps that perfection of appearance was the reason Betsy thought she would feel more comfortable if she wore the same type of clothing these girls did. But so far, she had been unable to second-guess them. If she came to school in casual attire, with western shirt and jeans, the triad wore their best plaid skirts and looked as if they planned to go to a party after school. On the other hand, if Betsy dressed up, the girls' casual attire made her feel overdressed.

Betsy's hair was as long as the three girls', and not far from the chestnut brown of Margo's. Now she tried parting it in the center and letting it sweep down so that sometimes it fell across her eyes. Betsy's hair was not trained to a center part. In fact, she had a small cowlick that made it fall into a side part, but she struggled with hairspray, vigorous brushing, and every variety of setting lotion she could find or concoct in the kitchen. Still, it was not entirely successful. Betsy wasn't even sure it was becoming.

"Why do you go against the natural tendency of your hair, Betsy?" her mother said. "It has such a lovely shine when you don't dull it with those preparations."

"But, Mother, you don't understand!" Betsy protested. "This is the way they wear it at Desertview High."

Her mother arched an eyebrow. "Does that mean that Betsy Alexander has to wear her hair that way?"

Betsy sighed. "I'm afraid so. I'm the newcomer. I want to be accepted."

Mrs. Alexander said nothing more, but Betsy had the feeling that she did not agree.

During that first week Betsy saw Pete often, passing him in the corridor as she moved from class to class. He always said "hi," and once he stopped her long enough to say, "Did you see that sunset last night? Wow! I'll bet you didn't have anything like that back East."

There were so many answers Betsy could have made to that, like, So what's one grungy sunset compared to green trees and grass everywhere, and a big lake!

But a wide grin spread Pete's mouth like he thought he was the one who had invented the sunset. Betsy shrugged her shoulders and hurried on. The warning bell for the next class had rung anyway, so she couldn't have lingered even if she had wanted to.

As she hurried on to her next class, she tried to think what the lovely Stacy, Pete's girl, might have replied. But Stacy hadn't lived in Chicago. She probably thought the desert was super, just the way Pete did.

By Saturday Mr. Alexander, with what help Betsy could give during the daylight hours after school, had the campground ready to take care of a limited number of campers. Early that morning Betsy dressed in her oldest, worn-out jeans and a faded T-shirt so that she could tackle more jobs to make the campground attractive. Mrs. Alexander insisted she felt well enough to greet would-be customers and show them to suitable sites. This left both Betsy and her father free to work full time.

At breakfast Betsy said, "Since first impressions are important, I'm going to brighten up the entrance." She told her parents she had found a large bucket of whitewash in one of the sheds behind the house. "I'm going to whitewash those stone gateposts. That way they'll stand out against all the"— she caught herself in time from saying drabness —"the brown of the desert. People can see where the campground is."

"Good idea," her father said. "Need some help?"

Betsy shook her head. "Thanks anyway. It'll be my project."

"I'll soon be able to start my cactus garden," her mother said. "That will add interest, and color when they bloom."

Betsy got up and began taking the empty plates to the kitchen where all three Alexanders washed and dried the dishes. Her mother liked to do what she could, but her strength was still limited. Betsy and her father conspired to take the burden of a task quietly between them without allowing her to feel like an invalid.

When the household chores were completed, Betsy went out to the gate with her bucket of whitewash and a large brush that she had found in the storage shed.

The sun was warm on her back, although there was a breeze that had enough coolness in it to remind her that autumn was at hand. She wondered if the leaves had begun to take on their fall colors back in Illinois. Then with a sigh she pushed that thought aside. She couldn't afford to indulge in such nostalgic thinking.

She set her bucket down and surveyed the posts she intended to whiten. Stones had been stacked one on top of another in such a clever way that they made very sturdy gateposts. The stones were of varying shades of reddish brown, quite attractive when viewed close up. In a way it seemed a shame to paint them white. But in their natural state they blended so perfectly with the desert landscape that nobody could see them until they were right upon them.

Betsy shrugged her shoulders. Why worry about a mere fifty or so stones when there must be millions more like them within a hundred-yard radius!

Her attention was diverted when a car pulling a large

trailer came along the road. The driver drew to a stop beside Betsy. The woman seated in the passenger's seat had graying hair, and Betsy saw that the man driving the car had only a fringe of white hair around his ears.

"Excuse me, Miss," the woman said. "But we're looking for a place to camp in our trailer. Do you know if there's a campground near?"

"Oh, yes." Betsy grinned widely at them. "You've come to the right place. It's here."

The man leaned across to peer beyond Betsy. "Here? I don't see any campers, and there's no sign."

"We just opened up." Betsy felt desperate now, the way she'd felt once when her father took her fishing, and she struggled to bring in the fish on her line. She mustn't let these people get away.

"We've got a few campsites ready, but my dad hasn't had time to put up a sign." She laughed. "We've been so busy, we just forgot. Won't you come look the place over?"

The couple turned to exchange a look, and the woman said, "After that last crowded place, it would be nice to have some peace and quiet."

"Now, Martha," the man said, "wait until you see what it's like before you commit yourself."

To Betsy's relief, however, he backed up and swung the car into the driveway. "Will you show us where to go, young lady?" he asked.

Betsy agreed eagerly, and she walked beside the driveway as the man followed slowly with his car and trailer.

Mrs. Alexander met them and took them on as Betsy lingered to watch. She was pleased when they took a campsite, backing the trailer in beside an overhanging pepper tree that would give them shade.

They were in business! Betsy thought as a wave of elation swept over her. She returned to her job, happier now.

She finished whitewashing one post and was standing back to admire its clean, fresh look when a couple drove up in a station wagon. At first she thought there must be more children hanging out the windows than there was space for them to sit inside. Closer inspection proved that there were only four small children, but their piping voices almost drowned out their parents' questions about the campground. Betsy put down her paintbrush to help these people find a campsite that would hold their large tent.

One of the children, a little boy probably near five years old, leaned far out the window and said in his shrill voice, "Are you a baby-sitter?"

Surprised, Betsy turned to him. "Why, yes, that is, I used to baby-sit, back in Chicago."

"Will you baby-sit us?"

Betsy laughed. "That's up to your parents." She doubted that there was any place to go around here, so they wouldn't need a baby-sitter. The parents were busy positioning the trailer in the campsite they had chosen, so they did not join in the discussion, probably had not even heard it. Betsy left them to return to her job.

Just as she began to work on the other gatepost, a jogger came into view along the road. As he approached her, Betsy saw that it was Pete Davis. He wore green jogging shorts, and the sun turned the light down on his arms to spun gold and made the perspiration-damp skin on his bare shoulders and back gleam like bronze. The long muscles in his legs stood out like thick cords. He slowed down and came to a stop directly in front of Betsy. "Hi," he said, not even out of breath.

"Hi," Betsy replied. "Do you do this often? I mean—" With a sweep of her hand she indicated the vast loneliness of the desert. There weren't any crossroads along the main highway that ran past the campground, and she felt that he might have run all the way from Borrego Springs.

Pete grinned. "Sure. I run every day. To keep in shape. You know. Track team."

She didn't know, but she was impressed. Then abruptly his friendly grin was swept away as he stared at something just behind her. A scowl of outrage twisted his features. "Did you do that?" he demanded, jabbing his hand out to point to whatever it was behind her that had captured his attention.

"Do what?" Betsy swung around to see what he was talking about. She couldn't see anything that might have caused such a change in him. "What did I do?"

"Did you—" His face turned red. "*Paint* those rocks?" His scathing tone made it sound worse than if she'd spread sticky tar on all the rocks in the desert.

"What rocks? Oh, you mean the gatepost. Well, it isn't exactly paint. It's only whitewash."

"Paint, whitewash, whatever, you're wiping out the beauty of the desert."

"But they're only rocks!"

"They blend all the colors of the desert. Part of its natural beauty. It's like defacing . . ."

"Look, I'm not hurting your desert. You've got miles of it out there. My family owns this part, including these rocks!"

"They're still part of the desert. Don't you care about preserving the beauty of the desert?"

Betsy longed to say, "What beauty?" But sudden, burning anger swept over her and she lashed out at him. "I care a lot more about my family's happiness! The way it is, nobody can even see this campground, and that means nobody will come here, and if that happens it'll tear up my family. Keeping us all together is what I really care about." The words had sounded strong and sure, but inwardly Betsy was shaking so hard she wondered why it didn't show in her voice. She had to defend her parents' project, even though being here made her more miserable every day. Before the churning emotions inside her could boil over into tears, she swung around and strode away from Pete, back down the driveway.

Her tennis shoes made only a light crunch on the gravel as she walked, and above the sound she heard the hum of a car's motor along the road. She was determined not to look back to see Pete's reaction to her outburst, but the sound of the car was too much to resist. It might be another camper looking for a place to spend the night, she thought. Besides, it gave her an excuse to turn around where she might be able to see how Pete reacted to her words.

What she saw made her breath catch in her throat, and the knot of anger burn unbearably in her stomach. There were three girls in the car as it pulled to a stop. One was tall and angular, one was dark and plump, and the third was a blond with a golden tan. It was this one, the one named Stacy, who leaned out the window and said in a mellow voice that was an invitation in itself, "Hi, Pete. Want a ride back to town?"

Pete didn't hesitate when he strode to the car. Betsy didn't hear his reply, but he slid in beside Stacy.

As the car swept away, she saw that Pete's arm lay across the back of the seat. Soon, she knew, it would slide down around Stacy's shoulders.

Watching them, Betsy thrust out her chin and said, very softly, "I'll paint every rock in this grungy desert if I want to, Pete Davis, no matter what you say." But before she went to the house, she brushed her arm across her face, wiping away the tears that somehow had found their way onto her cheeks.

Chapter Three

As Betsy approached the house she saw that her mother was sitting in the sunshine on the patio in front. Betsy knew she couldn't face her mother now, not in this angry, disturbed mood. So with a wave of her hand that she hoped made her look cheerful, she swung away into the path that led around to the storage shed. As she went she tried to sort out her own thoughts and feelings.

The stones that made up the gateposts might be prettier without whitewash, but the white attracted needed attention. After Pete's lecture, she wasn't about to change her plan.

Just wait until we get the campground fixed up, she thought. Then we'll see if Pete and his friends call it a dump!

She had finished whitewashing the first gatepost and was ready to start on the second. It was higher than the first. She would need something to stand on for extra height. She headed for the toolshed.

Her father was using the stepladder at the far end of the campground, trimming branches from the prickly thorn bush that threatened to take over one of the campsites. But she found a small, three-legged stool that would give her height.

She carried the stool back to the entrance, and with grim determination attacked the problem of whitewashing the second post.

She discovered quickly that the problem was not that the second gatepost was taller. It was because the ground dropped away sharply on the far side.

She began on the side nearest her, slapping her brush against the stones with a force that in her mind let Pete Davis know she refused to take his tongue-lashing meekly without protest. Slap! for Pete Davis. Slap! for his girl Stacy. Slap! Slap! Betsy began to enjoy her work, unleashing her anger. She slapped her brush so hard that some of the white sloshed over to splatter her. When she wiped it away with the sleeve of her shirt it left a white smudge against her cheek.

Then Betsy picked up the stool and set it firmly in the sandy soil. With the bucket of whitewash in one hand and the brush in the other, she stepped up onto the stool, teetering as she struggled to keep the bucket from spilling until she could regain her balance and step down. Setting the bucket on the ground, she eased a small stone under the sinking leg of the stool, then leaned on the stool to make sure it was steady. Then she picked up her tools again and stepped up onto the stool.

In the back of her mind she heard the gentle throb of a motor, but she was so intent on getting the stool set just right that she did not let the sound penetrate into her conscious thoughts.

Once again the stool tipped, this time one of its other two legs sinking into the sandy soil. With a sniff to express her exasperation, Betsy again stepped down, set aside her bucket and brush, and started to search for a stone that would fit under the stool's second leg.

A car door slammed behind her and a deep voice said, so close it made her swing around, "Hey, you need help in the worst way. A good thing I happened along."

Betsy found herself looking up into the grinning face of a person who must be somewhere in his late teens.

He looked like a cowboy who had stepped right out of a western movie, only Betsy didn't think that cowboys' clothes were so neatly pressed or that they had the unmistakable designer look. His boots were of the softest leather polished to a high gloss, with pointed toes and heels slanted inward to imitate the runover look. His tight-fitting trousers were tucked into the tops of his boots and held up by a handsome leather belt with a gleaming silver buckle. His shirt was of a soft shade of turquoise, as if to match his turquoise-and-silver watchband, and it was cut in the western style. The shade made his eyes and his hair that hung softly just above his collar appear blue-black against its brightness.

"Hey, I won't bite you," he said with a laugh as Betsy involuntarily backed away from him.

She was going about this all wrong, she thought with annoyance. Here was this exciting older man, whom she had all to herself, and what did she do but come across like a scared kid! It was all because of the grungy clothes she was wearing. Besides, she must have whitewash smeared over her from head to toe. With her sleeve she scrubbed at her face again.

He caught her hand in mid-motion. "Leave it, honey. On you, paint looks great; makes your eyes shine like polished turquoise."

Pete Davis would never say anything like that. If only he could see her now, with this older man. Stacy too. "Do you live around here?" she asked.

He laughed. "Don't let the get-up fool you, sweetheart. I'm no bronco buster. I'm strictly a city boy. Dudley deShon. My dad's deShon Plastics."

The way he said it made Betsy feel that she should recognize instantly the name or the company, or whatever, but she didn't. "Oh," she said. "Do you work for your dad?"

"Me? No way!" He pulled the corners of his mouth down. "No, love. I've just been riding my trusty steed there." A jerk of his head indicated the car nearby, a

Porsche of gleaming fire engine red. Betsy's eyes widened in spite of her determination to be cool. "Galloping across the desert in search of a fair maiden to rescue. And I see that I've come to the end of my quest. You are obviously in distress, and I'm here to help you." He reached down to grab the brush she had been using. "I can reach the top without having to resort to that abominable milking stool."

"Milking stool?" Betsy couldn't suppress her giggling. "It does look like something from an old movie. But you mustn't—not in those good clothes." She reached out to take the brush from him, moving toward him at the same time.

The bucket of whitewash stood on the ground between them, and in her rush to prevent him from getting whitewash on his handsome outfit, she stumbled over the bucket, not quite upsetting it but sloshing the liquid in it until some of it spilled out and spread over his highly polished boots.

"Oh, no!" she cried. "Now I've ruined your boots!"

"Think nothing of it, baby. There are plenty more where these came from."

"But they must cost—"

He laid a finger against his lips. "Shh! Didn't I tell you my old man is deShon Plastics? The price of a lousy pair of boots is mere peanuts." He snapped his fingers as an emphasis to his words.

Betsy insisted on taking him to her house to see if her mother could do something to remove the whitewash from the leather.

Dudley shrugged his shoulders. "Well, why not? It's for sure there's no excitement anywhere else in this dismal desert. What have I got to lose?" He took possession of her hand and swung along beside her as she hurried toward the house.

When they reached the patio, Betsy made short work of introducing him to her mother. "Mom, this is Dudley deShon, you know, of deShon Plastics, and

I've just ruined his handsome boots unless you know of something that will take whitewash off."

Mrs. Alexander looked horrified, but she produced a rag quickly and began to dab at the spots on the boots. "It's a good thing they're so highly polished," she said. "A lot of it will wipe off. They're such beautiful boots, it would be a shame to ruin them."

"Forget it," Dudley said. "If your daughter hadn't made a fuss about it, I wouldn't have bothered you. By the way, ma'am, your daughter is very persuasive." His wide mouth stretched in a smile. "She's beautiful too, as I'm sure you know."

"Well, of course her father and I think so, but then we may be prejudiced."

"You have every right to be," Dudley said.

Betsy's mother looked up from where she was rubbing at his boots. "I'm glad you can see Betsy's beauty," she said with a smile.

Betsy squirmed uncomfortably. It was pleasant to be told she was beautiful. This older man seemed to know his way around. On the other hand, being the focus of their remarks, as if she couldn't hear, was embarrassing. "I believe most of the white is coming off," she said. "Isn't it, Mom?"

"Don't worry if it doesn't," Dudley said. "I'm due for a new pair anyway. Tired of those."

"Betsy, I think there's some of your lemonade in the fridge," Mrs. Alexander said. "I'm sure Mr. deShon would like something cool as much as I would."

"Lemonade?" Dudley looked surprised. "Why, that would be fine. I haven't been offered plain, old-fashioned lemonade in a long time. It'll give me an excuse to sit for a while and visit with you two charming ladies."

The drawl in his words made Betsy glance at him quickly, but his face showed no sign that he was putting them on, and Mrs. Alexander was obviously delighted with his flattery. There was no doubt that it gave Betsy's wounded ego a much-needed lift. Humming softly, she hurried into the house.

When she returned, her mother and Dudley were discussing the campground, and Mrs. Alexander was explaining that they had just opened it for a few campers and hoped to have more as they readied more spaces.

When the three of them were settled with frosty glasses of lemonade, Dudley leaned back in his chair and set one ankle on top of the other knee in a relaxed pose. "You know, maybe there is something to this desert after all," he said, looking straight at Betsy. "I don't know when I've felt so relaxed. Maybe this is what I've been searching for."

"You're not in school?" Mrs. Alexander asked. "I thought maybe you were a college student."

Dudley's mouth turned down in a grimace. "I tried that route, UCI, USC. I even tried a couple of colleges back East, but it didn't work. Of course my dad hopes I'll join him in the business, but that's dull city. Now, out here, I'm beginning to feel free. Maybe this is what I want."

The hint of a frown drew a faint line between Mrs. Alexander's eyebrows. "What would you do in the desert? What kind of work?"

"Mother," Betsy interrupted. "That's just the point. Dudley is searching for the right place. He doesn't know yet what it will be." As she said the words, she wondered if they sounded dumb. Maybe she hadn't caught his meaning the way she thought she had.

Dudley set his glass down and reached over to press Betsy's hand with his own. "Exactly, Betsy. You get my message the way nobody else ever has."

Betsy smiled, but she could feel the warmth steal up over her face and she didn't dare glance at her mother. She was afraid there might be disapproval showing on her face. Betsy was so thrilled to find that she could communicate with this older man that she couldn't bear to risk having her mother disapprove. After all, there was nothing, really, to disapprove. Dudley had been nothing but polite and courteous from the minute she had first met him.

"I'll tell you what I'm going to do. Betsy, you said there were a couple of campsites ready to be occupied, and they weren't all taken yet. If you ladies will see that one of them is reserved for me, I'll just run into Borrego Springs and pick up some camping gear, then I'll come back and settle down for a couple of weeks right here. Okay?"

"Well, I—" Mrs. Alexander began with some hesitation.

At the same time Betsy said, "That'll be super, Dudley! I'll see that nobody takes the best campsite in the whole park."

Dudley turned to look directly at Mrs. Alexander as he said, "Don't worry about the money, ma'am." He stood up and from a small pocket in his tight trousers he fished out a roll of bills that made Betsy's eyes bulge. He peeled off several and handed them to Mrs. Alexander. "This ought to do as a deposit. We can settle up later."

Mrs. Alexander looked down at the bills in her hand. "Oh, you don't need to leave this much," she said.

Dudley leaned over and gently closed her hand over the bills. "Think nothing of it," he said, then turned to go. "I'll see you charming ladies later."

When he had gone and they heard the Porsche's motor throb into life, Betsy said, "Oh, Mom, isn't he fantabulous!"

Mrs. Alexander drew in a deep breath and slowly exhaled it. "Well, I must say he's unusual." Her eyes sharpened as she looked at Betsy. "But don't get any ideas, young lady. Dudley deShon is too old for you."

"Oh, Mo-*ther!* I've only just met him. I'm not planning to marry him."

"One never knows," Mrs. Alexander said. "One never knows."

Annoyed, Betsy all but leaped out of her chair and began to gather up the glasses. In the kitchen she rinsed them and set them in the sink to be washed with the evening's dishes. There were times when it was all she could do to keep from lashing out in anger at her mother. She had to remind herself sternly of her promise to cooperate fully until her mother's recovery was complete.

She was thankful that her mother did not join her in the kitchen, and when she had left it neat again she went out the back door and returned to her job of whitewashing the gatepost.

The scene with her mother had left raw ends on her nerves. Her mother didn't really understand her. But Dudley did. They had so much in common. Dudley was trying to find himself, and he had made Betsy realize that she too lacked a focus for her life. She hated the desert, yet she couldn't go back to Chicago. But with Dudley to help her she knew she would find a way to show her mother that she was mature, to make people like her and respect her, and know that she wasn't a piece of trash from the dump.

Wouldn't it be neat if Pete Davis could see her hurrying out of Desertview High to meet Dudley who stood waiting beside his Porsche and maybe kiss her on the mouth right there in front of everyone!

She allowed her fantasy to run on so that in her imagination she could see Stacy, Margo, and Tina watching her with envy. Wouldn't that put Pete Davis in his place too! She'd show Pete that not everyone was as uptight about whitewashing stone gateposts as he was!

Chapter Four

Betsy spent the remainder of the morning helping her father clear another campsite. Already the spaces they had made ready had been taken, and Mr. Alexander wanted to make sure they wouldn't have to turn down another source of income just because they hadn't cleared a space. While he trimmed the bushes that threatened to take up all the room, Betsy gathered up the cuttings, putting them into huge garbage bags to be taken later to the refuse area. When they had the space cleared of trash, Betsy would rake the sand and gravel that formed the soil until it was smooth and neat-looking. Then they intended to outline each campsite with rocks.

"I don't know when we'll get around to clearing away that old ruin," Mr. Alexander said. "I know it's unsightly but as long as people want to camp here we'll have to provide whatever spaces we have."

Betsy knew his reasoning made sense, but she wished they could get rid of the unsightly ruin so that the kids at school would stop calling it the dump.

She had taken Dudley deShon at his word, expecting him to return from Borrego Springs with some "camping gear," as he had said, and which she interpreted to mean a sleeping bag and possibly a tent. She was completely dumbfounded when just before noon she recognized the driver of the large and shining motor home as Dudley himself. Fastened onto the rear of the vehicle with a trailer hitch was a stripped-down chassis with little more to make it safe or comfortable to ride in than roll bars and a molded plastic bathtub-like seating space. Betsy knew that these wide-tired dune buggies were considered the only way to travel off road in the desert, but she couldn't imagine them being comfortable. Nevertheless, the whole outfit must have cost him a fortune, even if he had only rented the vehicles.

When Dudley pulled to a stop in front of her house, she walked over and tilted her head so that she could look up into his grinning face as he leaned out the window. "You don't believe in roughing it, do you?" she said, laughing.

"You don't think I'd settle for tent camping, do you?"

"Well, no, I guess you wouldn't."

"If I thought for a minute my Porsche would make it out into the open desert, I wouldn't have left it in that guy's care while I tooled off with this thing." A jerk of his head indicated the dune buggy. "But just remember, doll, we're going to explore the open desert."

"We?"

"Well, naturally. You're what makes the desert for me, sweetheart. I wouldn't stay here another minute if it weren't for you. Of course you're going with me."

Betsy couldn't help being pleased that this older man wanted to be with her so much that he was making a place for himself here in Shelter Valley. And yet, at the back of her mind was a nagging doubt. Pete Davis had warned her that venturing out into the open desert, off the established roads could be dangerous if you didn't know the desert.

She pushed the doubt aside. Pete didn't know Dudley deShon. Anyone could tell that Dudley would make out all right anywhere, in any situation. No one with the confidence, the know-how that Dudley had, could get into trouble in the desert or anywhere else. She pictured the look of astonishment on Pete's face when he saw her with Dudley. Even his girl Stacy would be impressed when she saw Betsy with Dudley deShon.

"Just let me settle in, love," Dudley said. "And then you and I can roll out the old dune buggy and see what it'll do in the open desert."

"The open desert?" She was stalling. She knew it.

"Sure. That's what those wheels are made for, sand rolling. Now let's not waste any more time talking about it. It's action that we want."

Still Betsy hesitated, wishing at the same time that she could just forget everything else and go with Dudley. "I was clearing another campsite with my dad," she said. "He's counting on me—"

"Ah, take a break, sweetheart. You've done your thing for today, whitewashing those posts." His eyes glittered with a conspiratorial light. "After all, if it hadn't been for you, I wouldn't have thought about spending one night in this desolate place, let alone signing up for two weeks! Your old man owes you a commission in time off if nothing else."

Betsy's spine stiffened and she frowned at him. "We don't work that way. All of us in our family cooperate without any thought of who owes who what."

His easy grin reassured her. "Aw, baby, I was only kidding. But I'm serious about kidnapping you for a couple of hours to try out this dune buggy. Just give me time to back the motor home into its space."

He had a way of talking her out of being mad at him. She couldn't stay angry for long around Dudley because he made her feel good.

With a casual wave of his hand he drove away along the driveway that led into the campground proper. Betsy stood watching him, a thoughtful half-smile on her face. As he reached the campsite, she saw her father cross from the other side of the campground and come up to talk to Dudley through the open window of the motor home. For a few minutes they talked together, and then Mr. Alexander began to guide him as he eased the big vehicle into the parking space. Apparently her father accepted Dudley, Betsy thought with a small sigh of relief. Well, why shouldn't he? Dudley was attractive and polite, he had paid his fee, and they needed all the campers they could attract to make the campground a success. Dudley had everything going for him.

She started toward the house to help her mother prepare lunch, but before she reached her destination, a light crunch of gravel on the drive, not heavy enough to be a car, caught her attention. She turned toward the sound and saw that Pete Davis was wheeling along the driveway on his bicycle.

"Hi, Betsy," he called out as if the earlier unpleasantness had not erupted between them. Then with complete good humor he said, "I'm not giving up on convincing you that the desert's rocks are something special."

He had come up even with her and he swung off his bike, still holding the handlebars as he grinned at her.

"Oh?" Betsy said, wondering if he intended to suggest that she somehow take the whitewash off the gateposts.

"Yeah. Get your bike and we can ride over to Sand Point. From there it's only a short hike up the dry wash to where you can see some petroglyphs."

"Petroglyphs?"

"Yeah. Indian picture writing. These are maybe hundreds of years old, and not many people know about them. But I thought you'd like to see them. It'll help you understand how really great the desert is. Come on. I've got our lunch. Let's go while the light's just right."

"Now?"

"Well, sure." His grin faded abruptly. "You won't

hold that blowup we had this morning against me, will you?"

"Well, no, but, well, you see, I was helping Daddy clear another campsite so we could take on more campers." She was saying the same words to Pete, using the same excuse she had used with Dudley, and somehow it made her feel uncomfortable. But it wasn't just an excuse, she reminded herself. It was the truth. "We haven't finished it yet and—"

"Hey, sweetheart, what'd I tell you!" The words, spoken from behind her, made Betsy wince. Trouble, she knew, was approaching in the person of Dudley deShon.

"It's all set," Dudley said as he came up behind Betsy to rest his hands on her shoulders. "Your dad agreed with me that you need some time to have fun, and that I'm the guy to help you have it."

Pete's eyebrows had drawn together and his face was slowly turning red. "Betsy, I thought you had to—"

As if Dudley had just noticed Pete, he said, "Oh, hi," in a pleasant tone, interrupting him. Then as Dudley moved around Betsy to encircle her with his arm he said to Pete, "I'm afraid you'll have to excuse my girl now, young man. Betsy and I have plans for the rest of the day." He gave her shoulders a squeeze as if to emphasize his words.

Betsy saw a flash of anger in Pete's gray eyes and said, "I really did mean to finish the job with my dad, Pete, but—"

"But I persuaded Mr. Alexander to let her go," Dudley finished her sentence. "I'm Dudley deShon." He offered his hand. "What'll I call you?"

Pete did not shake hands. Instead, he glared directly at Dudley and said, his mouth twisting into a sneer, "Just call me a sucker." With a swish of gravel, he flung his bike around, leaped onto it and wheeled away down the driveway. As he skidded around the curve into the main road, gravel spurted from the tires.

Dudley turned to give Betsy a raised eyebrow look. "Now what do you suppose was cracking his cool?"

"Maybe he didn't like your attitude," Betsy said, not sure that she had either.

"Look, doll. If he really cared about you, like the way I do, he wouldn't have given up so quickly. Now, would he?"

Betsy had to admit that she agreed with him. She reminded herself also that at least Dudley didn't call her home a dump the way Pete's friends did, or try to make her like the desert as Pete did. She was lucky that Dudley had come along, and she had better be grateful that he cared enough about her to stay here awhile. She would do everything she could to make him want to stay even longer.

"Come on, doll;" Dudley said. "Ready to take off?"

"Just a minute, Dudley. I have to tell my mother something." Before he could question her, she slipped from his embrace and ran along the driveway, through the patio, and up the two steps that led into the house. "Mom!" she called from the front door. "What's for lunch today?"

"You must be really hungry, and I guess working so hard does whet your appetite," her mother said. "I'll make tuna salad if you'll chop up the celery for me." She turned from the kitchen counter where she was standing, to glance at Betsy. When their eyes met, Mrs. Alexander frowned slightly. "Is something wrong, dear? Your face is flushed and . . ."

"Nothing's wrong, Mom," Betsy said with an attempt at a relaxed laugh. "It's just that, well, I was wondering if maybe I could ask Dudley to eat with us?"

"The boy on the bicycle? I saw you talking . . . Oh. Dudley. That's the young man who brought the motor home in, isn't it?" Her eyes searched Betsy's face.

Betsy nodded, wondering what her mother might

have read in her expression. Parents always thought they could read your innermost thoughts. The bad part was that sometimes it was weird the way they hit it right.

"I'm always glad to welcome your friends into our home, dear," Mrs. Alexander went on after only the briefest pause. "But you've known him such a short time. You know, we can't invite just every camper who comes to stay here into our home. We'd never have any privacy, or make any profit."

"Mother," Betsy said through stiff lips. "Dudley isn't just *any* camper. After all, his father is deShon Plastics."

"I know, dear. And it's fine that he can be proud of his family. But what about Dudley himself? What do you know about him?"

With a lift of her chin Betsy said, "I know he's a great guy, and you saw what good manners he has. That should have impressed you." She hadn't meant the words to sound all that nasty. On the other hand, she wasn't a dumb little kid who couldn't judge the qualities of people she wanted for friends but had to have Mommie decide which ones she could play with.

Her mother didn't appear to be upset by her thrust. "I know he has nice manners," Mrs. Alexander said, "and if you really want to invite him for lunch, that's good enough for me. You have excellent judgment, Betsy, but make sure you're honest with yourself. Dudley is considerably older than you. Enjoy your youth and your contemporaries while you can. You've plenty of time to become involved with older men later."

Betsy let her lips curl in scorn. "You talk like I'm about to have an affair with Dudley, Mom." Then with a twitch of her shoulders and a smug smile she went on, "Actually, all I plan to do is to ride around the desert in his dune buggy with him. Do you *mind?*"

Mrs. Alexander's smile was bland, as if she hadn't caught the jibe. But Betsy knew she had when her mother said, "You are old enough to make your own decisions, Betsy. I won't stand in your way. And I know you'll remember that getting lost in the desert is not only easy, it is life threatening. I hope your young man will stay on the established roads." Then, as if there had been no friction between them, she said, "Now why don't you go and call in your father and Dudley. By the time they have washed up we'll have this salad made and the ice tea poured."

Before Betsy went to call in the men she let her eyes sweep over her mother's face. There was no anger there, but it seemed to Betsy that the shadows had deepened under her eyes. Her mother's recovery had been slow but steady since they came to the desert, but now, Betsy thought as her own heart twisted inside her, I've made it harder for her to relax and get the rest she needs. Why did I have to blow my cool that way with her?

The answer was clear. Her own problems had blinded her to those of her mother. Dudley had been right. She needed to get out and away. Her disposition was all shot. She needed this afternoon of freedom with Dudley deShon.

Chapter Five

The family lunch, which included Dudley, was a complete success, Betsy thought. Dudley seemed to outdo himself in his effort to be charming and entertaining. He kept all of them laughing with tales of his adventures, and seemed able to converse with ease on many subjects. Even Mrs. Alexander appeared to fall under his spell.

When they had finished eating, Dudley insisted on helping Betsy with the clearing up, but his efforts were so awkward that at last Mrs. Alexander said, laughing, "Dudley, I'm afraid domesticity is not your most admirable trait. But you've made me feel so much better with your amusing stories that I feel quite able to clear away the lunch things." She sent the two of them on their way, only cautioning them against getting lost in the desert.

They went outside and climbed into the dune buggy, and Dudley started the motor. With a swish of gravel he drove out of the driveway. As Betsy turned to wave to her mother who stood on the patio watching them go, gratitude flooded through her. On the whole, her parents were really okay. In a pinch they could be counted on to be on her side.

Once on the main road, Dudley increased the dune buggy's speed, and the wind blew in over the windshield and in from the sides to make her hair fly. The sun was bright and so warm that she couldn't help thinking smugly that back in Chicago, the wind off the lake would be so cold and would cut like a knife this late in the autumn.

Above the rush of the wind and the roar of the dune buggy's motor, Betsy had to shout to be heard, but Dudley's deep voice carried easily and he did most of the talking. He kept her amused, telling her more stories of his own experiences. These were not the same mild, impersonal anecdotes as those with which he had amused her parents. Betsy silently applauded him for his discretion. He made her feel more his equal when he told her, for instance, about his attempts at acquiring a college education. These attempts had been brief and sporadic. One in particular had been disappointing to him, but Dudley made his account of it sharply amusing.

"I chose that college because I liked the name," he said. "The College of the Sequoias. It sounded cool and woodsy." A wry grin twisted his mouth. "It's in Visalia." He drew the word out, using the long *i* and *a*, and rumbling the *z* sound of the *s* that followed them. "Ever been to Visalia?"

Betsy shook her head. "No."

"You haven't missed much." He threw back his head and laughed. "There's not a sequoia tree within fifty miles of the college. And as far as cool goes, that day in September you could fry an egg on the sidewalk. When the power went out all over town from overuse of air conditioning, I packed up and left. I'd had all I wanted of that school."

"You mean you just gave up? Hadn't you already enrolled?"

He shrugged. "Sure, I'd enrolled. I'd given them a fat chunk of cash. But I couldn't take that heat long enough to try to get a refund." He shrugged. "Anyway, why bother? It'd be only pocket change to my old man. It was his problem."

NEVER SAY NEVER

The money wasn't what Betsy had had in mind when she asked the question, but his reply left her a little awestruck. Already her own parents were planning and trying to put money aside for her college education, even though this move and her mother's doctor bills made it doubly hard. "Did you try another college?" she asked.

"Naa. I had to find myself. I took some time out, traveling." He had wandered around Europe, and moved on to the Near East, searching for—Betsy wasn't quite clear about what he was searching for, but he made it plain that finding it was all important to him.

"You know, sweetheart," he began as his hand left the wheel to grasp hers. "Maybe it's right here in the desert after all."

Betsy's heart raced. Did he mean what she hoped he meant, that she might be the answer to his search? This was a little more than she knew how to answer, so she took advantage of a sign that appeared along the edge of the road. "Well of Eight Echoes," she read. "Let's stop, Dudley, and see what that could be. It's right up ahead, the sign says."

He swerved the dune buggy to the side of the road and drew to a stop. They both climbed out and walked the few yards over the sandy soil to a cleared space where a rusty pipe thrust itself up out of the ground.

"It doesn't look very impressive," Dudley said.

Betsy agreed more or less, although she didn't say so. Her curiosity was piqued, and she went over to examine the pipe. By bending over a little she could put her mouth close to the pipe's opening. "Hello!" she called down.

The answer came back in a series of hollow sounds, "o-o-o-o—" that all blended into each other.

"I couldn't count if there were eight, could you, Dudley?"

"Naa. There might have been more than eight, or less." He bent over and picked up a pebble from the ground. Before Betsy could stop him, he went to the pipe and dropped the pebble into its opening.

"Dudley!" she cried. "If everyone dropped a pebble, after a while they'd fill up the well and there wouldn't be any echo left."

"So what?"

"It's much more fun to throw your voice down there than a stone."

His eyes hardened. "Look, Betsy, if you're going to lecture me, I can get my kicks somewhere else. And I will, too." He stomped back toward the dune buggy.

Panic threatened to paralyze Betsy. She couldn't let him go away now, even before the other kids at school, especially the three girls Mr. Logan had called the triad, had seen that she could attract an older man. She said quickly, "Oh, Dudley, I didn't mean to lecture you. Come on, this well's a drag anyway. Let's find something more exciting."

She ran after him, catching up just before he reached the dune buggy. She smiled at him. "I'm sorry, Dudley. I'm ready now to do what you want."

"That's my girl," he said and brushed his lips over her hair. His good humor had been restored as they climbed into the dune buggy and drove on along the main road.

Several miles farther on, he swung the dune buggy off the main road and onto a dirt road that showed little use.

"Hey," she said. "Where are you going?"

"I told you we'd explore the desert. You said you were ready to do what I want, didn't you?"

Betsy shifted in the molded plastic seat. She had said that. But she had also promised her mother that she would see that they didn't get lost in the desert. "Do you know where this road goes?" she asked.

"Of course not. It wouldn't be exploring if I did, would it?"

So far, they were safe, Betsy thought. As long as they followed the track one way, they could follow it back. But the thought had hardly formed in her mind when Dudley discovered a canyon leading off the road.

"Hey," he said. "Let's see how good these wide tires really are in a sandy stream bed." He swung off the unpaved road and into the canyon.

Betsy was silent, her thoughts busy trying to find a way to persuade him to return to the marked roadways without driving him away from her forever.

The canyon's walls rose higher to either side of them as they made their way deeper and deeper into its shadowy depths, and the walls seemed to close in on them as the canyon grew more narrow. When at last they were halted by a huge boulder that blocked the passage, Betsy felt a a distinct relief. At least she was certain they could find their way back from here.

Dudley swore under his breath, but quickly his mood brightened. "Okay, let's get out and see what the place has to offer."

Betsy sprang out of the dune buggy and stood looking up beyond the steep, high walls of the canyon, to the small patch of sky visible from where they stood. The sky appeared so deeply blue she thought for an instant that darkness was approaching. After only a second's panic, she realized that it was the shaded canyon that made it seem that way.

But a new uneasiness stole over her as Dudley's face appeared suddenly closer to her own and she realized that he was bending over her. For an instant his lips met hers, but suddenly the loneliness of the little canyon, the sense of being shut off here with this older, more experienced man, overwhelmed her. She sprang back away from him and cried, "Oh, look, Dudley. What is that? It looks like—" She ran to where two boulders stood to form a small pocket of the angle between them. In the soft sand that made the floor of this pocket, four pieces of wood jutted up at regular angles to each other so that, with their shadows, they formed a perfect fan pattern against the sand. "Those things look as if they're man-made, not as if they grew there."

"So what if they are? Hey, doll, what's with you? I thought you liked me as much as I like you."

"Oh, I do, Dudley. I like you a lot. It's just that . . . Well, we're out here so far from everything and, well, I just . . ." How could she explain an uneasiness so vague that she didn't understand it herself?

He raised one eyebrow as he looked at her. "Don't tell me you're one of those kids that's never been kissed?"

"Oh, no. I've been kissed." Betsy felt the hot blood rise from her neck up into her face and she hated herself for blushing. In her discomfort she took a step sideways and stumbled into a creosote bush.

A jack rabbit, obviously startled out of its hiding place, sprang out from behind the bush and with great, flying leaps covered the ground and quickly disappeared in the distance.

The effect on Dudley was startling. He threw back his head and burst into laughter. In between peals of laughing, he said, "That's it. You're like that jack rabbit. Scared into running. So old Dudley's the big, bad wolf, is he? Hey, Dudley, old man, how does that grab you? Not bad, eh?"

He was laughing at her, and Betsy felt a flash of anger. She drew herself up and said, "It wasn't you I was scared of, it was the desert. Now, you can take me home. I've had enough of exploring for today."

He shrugged. "Okay. It's still early enough for me to find excitement somewhere else. If that's the way you want it."

Panic hit Betsy like a blow. Did that mean he would take his motor home and leave the campground, leave Shelter Valley? When she hadn't even had a chance to show the triad girls that she could attract an older man? And when her father had counted on the rent from that space for two whole weeks? Mr. Alexander of course would insist on returning the unused part of Dudley's fee. How could she face everyone if she let such a thing happen?

On the other hand, Betsy couldn't bring herself to back down on her stand. She couldn't imagine herself saying, "I've changed my mind, Dudley. You may kiss me now."

In silent misery Betsy walked back to the dune buggy and climbed in. Although she hadn't even glanced back, she knew that Dudley was following her.

The ride back to the Sagebrush RV Park was spent in silence. Now the wind seemed to have a chill as it caught Betsy's hair, and the sun was sinking toward the hazy purple mountains in the far distance. It lacked its earlier comforting warmth.

Dudley let her off in the driveway, and as soon as she had jumped down, he swung the dune buggy around and roared back out to the main road. Well, at least he hadn't taken his motor home away. He must plan to spend at least one more night in the campground. But there was only small comfort in that thought for Betsy, and she dreaded having to face her parents when she went in. She knew they would ask if she had enjoyed her outing with Dudley. Then what would she say? What could she say?

Betsy Alexander, you are a nerd, a total nerd, a silly grunge, she told herself silently. She had acted like a dumb junior high kid, longing for her first kiss yet afraid because she didn't know how to respond.

If it had been Pete Davis, a small voice deep inside her tried to argue.

Betsy fought down the voice. Pete wasn't Dudley. Dudley was older, more exciting, and he had his own money, plenty of it. Why, he could marry her right now if he wanted to, and take her away from this horrendous desert.

The thought suddenly made a hot flame dart up Betsy's spine. Hadn't she flared up when she thought her mother was implying that she might be getting too serious about Dudley? And now her thoughts were running right along that dangerous path. Deep in her heart, Betsy knew that it would be a long time before she would want to marry anyone. But she couldn't help it if her problems were so bad they made her try to escape through fantasies. In any case, she was sure of one thing, that the next time Dudley deShon made a pass at her she wouldn't jump away like some wild thing out here in the desert. This very night she'd practice in front of her mirror until she found just the right approach, the right way to show that she was willing for him to kiss her but not too eager so that she would seem dumb.

She had been walking steadily toward the house as these daydreams played across her mind, but she wasn't aware of how far she had come until her mother's voice interrupted her.

"Well, you're home earlier than I expected, Betsy. Did you have a nice time with Dudley?"

She came to with a start, and her heart seemed to plummet all the way down to her toes. This was what she had expected, but she hadn't prepared for it. "Uh," she said, "yes, but it was getting kind of chilly out there, so we came back." Without waiting for her mother's reply, not wanting to get involved in a discussion that would reveal more than she wanted to, Betsy hurried on to the bathroom, hoping her mother would think she had to go in the worst way.

Betsy didn't sleep well that night. She lay awake for a long time and finally, restless beyond endurance, slid out of bed and padded across the rather worn loop carpeting to the window. Kneeling on the floor, she rested her elbows on the low sill and gazed out into the night. Never had she known such complete darkness. The campground lay several miles outside of Shelter Valley, and her room faced away from the town. Without street lights or other artificial lighting, the darkness was complete.

After a few minutes her eyes adjusted, and she could see far in the distance the darker bulk of mountains against the star-lit sky. The stars! She gasped as she realized how very many there were here, and how bright they appeared against the dark sky. Now it didn't seem like a cliché to say the sky looked like a great display of diamonds. Her hand reached out, as if they were so close she could touch them.

Was this one of the things Pete meant when he said there was so much beauty in the desert? But you couldn't go wandering around in all this darkness, not without some kind of light, and that would spoil the effect.

Far in the distance a dog began to bark. At least, that was what Betsy first thought it was. But then the barking rose to an eerie, plaintive howling that was repeated from one direction and another until it seemed that every hill within hundreds of miles reverberated with the ghostly sound. Icy shivers ran along her spine. It sounded like creatures straight out of that horror movie she had seen in Chicago. Pete could have his desert, she thought. She'd go along with Dudley deShon. The desert was dismal!

The howling faded gradually off into the distance, but it left Betsy thinking of Dudley. His dune buggy had not returned when darkness settled over the campground, and although she had listened for the distinctive sound of its motor in the driveway, she had not heard it since. Maybe he had just taken off and left the motor home here. The money that would cost him wouldn't mean anything to him. What if she never saw him again? Betsy ran back to her bed, flung herself onto it, and buried her head in her pillow. She didn't cry, but she felt like it. Her life was really messed up now, and everything she did seemed to make things worse.

At last, she heard the dune buggy's motor and the crunch of gravel under its wide tires. Dudley had come back. With a great sigh of relief, she fell asleep.

Even then, her sleep was disturbed by strange dreams. In one of them Pete Davis kept sending her messages in Indian picture writing. Betsy could not decipher the messages, but when she took them to Dudley deShon he became furious and tore up the papers before Betsy could grab them away from him. Betsy lashed out at him. "My dad will be furious with you for doing this!"

In her dream, Dudley only shrugged and said, "Why should I care? My old man is deShon Plastics."

She woke to find herself tangled in her sheets, her bed a mess. She got up and without turning on the light smoothed the sheets and remade her bed before she sank back into it. The ancient Greeks' "rosy fingered dawn" had begun to color the sky before she fell asleep again.

Chapter Six

Next morning before Betsy went in to breakfast, she looked out the window where she could see the campsite occupied by Dudley's motor home. It was still there, and so was the dune buggy. She gave a huge sigh of relief. All her worries last night had been useless. Dudley hadn't left.

As she came into the living room she saw, through the sliding glass door, the dune buggy sweep up the driveway and skid around the curve into the main road. Sudden disappointment knotted in her stomach. Then she told herself that he was probably only going into town for breakfast. She was sure that Dudley deShon, whose father was deShon Plastics, wouldn't make his own breakfast even though his handsome motor home must have the finest kitchen available.

He could have eaten with us, she thought. But the thought was swallowed up in the realization that she had watched him turn away from the town of Shelter Valley. There was no town, no restaurant in that direction closer than the Mexican border. Undoubtedly Dudley was going to spend the day south of the border.

In the dining room her parents were already seated at the table. They greeted her with smiles, but Betsy had the distinct feeling that only seconds before she had entered the room they were discussing her. She wondered if they could have any idea of the problems that faced her.

After their greetings, her father said, "We can't actually waste a day, Betsy, but I thought since it's Sunday we'd vary our program, work on something different."

Betsy slid into her chair and helped herself from the platter of scrambled eggs her mother had put on the table. As she dropped a slice of bread into the toaster, she said, "Whatever you want, Dad. I'm available all day today. You'd better take advantage of my free day because it's school again tomorrow."

"How would you like to get started clearing away that old ruin out back?"

Betsy sat up straighter, feeling a smile curve her mouth. "Really? Can we take the time off from getting campsites ready for takers?"

Her father smiled. "We've both worked hard, and we've a couple of unoccupied sites that are in good shape. With the weekend over, we won't have many people coming to camp. I think we deserve a break, at least a change."

Betsy grinned widely. "I'll agree with that. And I'll enjoy getting rid of that mess." She dug into her breakfast with renewed enthusiasm.

"Well," her father drawled. "Don't expect miracles. It'll take us more than one day to make much of a showing there. That's a big pile of melted adobe, and it looks to me as if it's got a lot of trash in it. Old trash."

"You'll be surprised how fast I can work on this project," Betsy said.

Mrs. Alexander spoke up. "Your enthusiasm is contagious, Betsy. Maybe I'll come out for a little while and do what I can."

"Now, Sharon," Mr. Alexander chided. "You mustn't overtax yourself just when you're making such a good comeback."

"Don't worry, dear. I'll bring that campstool and sit while I sift. There just might be something valuable in all that trash."

Betsy made a face. "Like at the dump? I've heard that some people live off what they find in city dumps."

Mrs. Alexander smiled. "Well, who knows?"

After breakfast Betsy rose and began to clear away the dishes, but her mother stopped her. "I'll take my turn today. I feel absolutely great and you two will need all the time you can get to work on the ruin. Leave the housework for me this time."

"You're sure?" Mr. Alexander asked.

"Absolutely sure," she said with a smile as she tilted her head back for his kiss. "But you're a darling to be concerned."

They went outside and Mr. Alexander handed Betsy a shovel to carry while he pushed the wheelbarrow with his own larger shovel in it. They hurried to the heap of melted adobe in back of the house.

Betsy was thankful to get out of working in the kitchen with her mother this morning. She didn't feel up to facing their usual intimate talk when they worked together. Her father didn't probe into her innermost feelings the way her mother did. Betsy and her father had a warm relationship, one she sometimes felt was easier to handle than that with her mother. Not that she loved her mother any less. It was just that Mom had a way of seeing behind her words to the thoughts that sparked them. This sometimes, like now when she felt defensive about Dudley's rushing off without her, made her uncomfortable.

So now she felt almost lighthearted as she and her father went toward the old ruin.

When they reached the pile of rubble, they studied it from every side to plan how best to tackle the job they had to do. Mr. Alexander walked around it, measuring it with his eyes. On the far side, he said, "Look here, Betsy, there are some adobe bricks still intact. Looks like part of the wall of the building, a corner to be exact."

Betsy didn't really care much what shape the rubble took, but she went to see what her father meant. She saw that a corner of the building had indeed remained intact, and what remained of the mud and straw adobe had been blown by the wind or washed by heavy rains into a heap against this angled corner.

Her father leaned over the wall and with his fingers dug away at the dry, crumbling adobe until he had uncovered a broken piece of pottery. He picked up the shard and with his finger brushing away the soil that still clung to it, examined it closely. "Looks like part of an old wash basin," he said. He looked up and his gaze traveled out across the desert floor until he seemed to be looking beyond even the distant hazy mountains. "I remember a wash basin and pitcher that my grandmother kept on a marble-topped commode. Nobody used it anymore, because by then her house had plumbing and a modern bathroom. But it was pretty. Had a pattern of roses all over it."

"How would a thing like that get out here?" Betsy wondered.

He shrugged. "Who knows? Maybe someone moving his household out west brought it on the Butterfield Stage." With a thoughtful frown he looked at Betsy. "You know, maybe we'd better not just plunge into this heavy handed with our shovels. There just could be some valuable history buried in this mess."

Betsy laughed. "Don't tell me you're going to turn into an archaeologist, Daddy."

His laugh was lighter than hers had been. "Well, hardly that. I'd be strictly an amateur, and I've got to make a living for my family first. But seriously, Betsy, we don't want to do anything to destroy history."

"You sound like Mrs. Nesbit."

"Mrs. Nesbit?"

Betsy nodded. "The secretary in the office at school. She lights up like a game machine when she talks about history. Really." She didn't go into detail about how Mrs. Nesbit had said Betsy lived in the midst of history and not in a dump as the triad girls had hinted. What with that and Pete shoving his liking for the desert down her throat, and now Daddy going on like a broken piece of china was a gold nugget from a mine or something, Betsy had had enough.

While she was thinking these dark thoughts Mr. Caldwell, who had been camping with his wife and four small children in a tent in site three, came up with his youngest, Timmie. Mr. Caldwell was interested in what they were doing in the ruin, and he and Betsy's father began to talk about the old stagecoach run.

Timmie, of course, was not interested in this grown-up talk, and Betsy, feeling sympathy for him, began to talk to the toddler on his own level. They found a horned toad, so nearly the color of the sandy soil that he was almost invisible. She persuaded Timmie to stand very still so that they could watch the toad without frightening him away. Then when the toad grew more confident and began to move, Timmie laughed and tried to capture it. The toad escaped, disappearing into a clump of prickly weeds where Timmie could not follow.

When tears of disappointment threatened to burst from Timmie, Betsy asked his father's permission to take him to the small playground on the property and give him a turn on the swing.

"By all means, if you really want to," Mr. Caldwell said cheerfully. "I think Timmie was getting tired of my company."

Betsy settled him in the swing and pushed him high enough to make him squeal with delight but not so high that he would be in danger of falling out. After a time, however, Timmie said, "Where's my mommie?" He rubbed his eyes with his fist and said again, "Mommie," in a plaintive voice.

Betsy guessed it must be time for a nap. "Let's go find your daddy first, Timmie," she said. "He'll take you back to your tent and your mommie."

As they walked back, hand in hand, to the old ruin, the sound of a car behind them made Betsy swing around. She hoped it might be Dudley returning to make life interesting again for her. It wasn't Dudley. Instead, it was another family looking for a place to camp, and Betsy's father left Mr. Caldwell and went to take care of the new people.

As he walked away, he turned back and said with a grin, "Guess I was wrong about no campers after the weekend. We'd better work some more on the campsites and wait until we have time to sift through this ruin carefully."

Timmie said to his father, "Betsy swang me. Up to the sky."

Mr. Caldwell lifted Timmie up in his arms. "Betsy's a nice friend, isn't she, Timmie?" When Timmie nodded his head, Mr. Caldwell said to her, "You gave me a break too. Your dad and I got to talking about that old stagecoach and I forgot all about the time. Fascinating history here. I'd like to find out more about it."

Betsy smiled, but at the same time she sighed in mock despair. "You ought to get together with Pete Davis, this boy at my school. He's into Indian picture writing. Really."

"You don't care for local history, I take it?"

"Well, it's okay, I guess, but it seems kind of dead and gone. People are more interesting."

Mr. Caldwell grinned. "Don't you think that people made history?"

"I guess so, but I didn't know them. I didn't live back in those days."

Mr. Caldwell looked as if he wanted to argue the point, but Timmie interrupted, saying, "Mommie. I want my mommie."

"I guess the little guy's sleepy," Mr. Caldwell said. "I'll have to take him back. But I want to talk to you some more about the history of this place. I think you're underestimating it."

Maybe so, Betsy thought, but she didn't really care that much. She was glad Mr. Caldwell had had to leave. He was a nice man, really, when he wasn't pushing history the way everyone else seemed to be doing. What was this, a campaign to make Betsy

Alexander like living in the desert? Maybe when they got rid of that old ruin—if they ever did—they'd let her forget about history and get on with living today, the way Dudley deShon did.

Betsy stood for a few minutes after the two men and Timmie had gone. For once she was almost sorry to see the new campers. If it hadn't been for them, she and her father could have kept on working, and the pile of rubble might have been reduced a little by the end of today.

But of course that was not fair of her, she told herself. The Alexander family needed every bit of income they could get, and she was being not only selfish but also shortsighted by even allowing such thoughts to enter her mind.

Betsy spent the remainder of the day working hard, so hard that she left herself little time to think about Dudley and his rushing off or even of Pete Davis and how mad he had been when he left.

But when night came, and she was safely closed in her own room, she unleashed her imagination and indulged in fantasies. She made herself believe that Dudley would be waiting for her after school on Monday, and Pete would be standing on the sidewalk outside of the school, where he would watch her slide into the seat of Dudley's fiery red Porsche, for in her fantasy he had brought his own car back. At another place on the sidewalk, the three girls of the triad would also watch Betsy get in beside Dudley deShon and drive away.

But then something unexpected happened to the daydream, for suddenly one of the triad girls, Stacy, left the other two and ran over to throw herself into Pete's arms. As the Betsy in the fantasy glanced back over her shoulder, Pete's arms enfolded Stacy. Before the Porsche whisked Betsy away she heard Stacy say, "Don't let it grab you, Pete. After all, she's only the girl who lives at the dump."

Alone in her room, the real Betsy cried, "No!" as

she twisted with the agony of torment. How could her own imagination betray her so horribly!

Monday morning Betsy had to drag herself out of bed. She didn't want to go to school where she would have to face the triad and Pete Davis—and the scene of the fantasy that had betrayed her. On the other hand, she didn't want to stay at home where she would be reminded of Dudley. His motor home was in its usual place, but the dune buggy was not there. Again the question beat against Betsy's thoughts: Had Dudley gone away and left the motor home, never to return to it?

She decided that since she had to go to school she would dress to please herself for once. What did it matter whether or not the triad girls approved of her clothes, since they wouldn't like anything about her anyway. She would dress in an outfit that would make her feel as good as possible.

She chose the new knickers she had bought with baby-sitting money she'd saved from Chicago. With them she wore her favorite top, a turquoise confection in a synthetic fabric that was as fuzzy and soft as a favorite stuffed animal. She had chosen this color because it almost exactly matched her eyes and it made a perfect background for the rich chestnut of her hair. The texture of the blouse was something no girl who loved stuffed animals could resist. Just stroking it with gentle fingers made her feel better, and with its softness caressing her skin as she shrugged into it, the world looked brighter than it had before.

Betsy dreaded second period English this morning because not only was Pete Davis in the class, but also Tina, Margo, and Stacy. Since Betsy had to walk all the way from the far end of the building where her first period classroom was located, most of the others were already in their seats when she came into the room. Before she entered, she inhaled deeply and carefully raised her chin to what she hoped was a jaunty angle. Then she spread her lips in a smile, giving the impression that she knew some delicious secret.

NEVER SAY NEVER

Pete said "hi" to her as she passed his chair, and that almost made Betsy lose her cool. He didn't sound mad now. She was so surprised that she let her eyes widen and forgot to smile. Then she remembered in time and tried for a casual tone when she answered him. Her "hi" came out as a ragged sound, and she had to clear her throat and say the word again.

"Looked like your campground was almost full when I jogged past this morning," he said. "I'm glad."

"Thanks," was all she could manage, for again she was astonished that he seemed to have forgotten how angry he was at her. But then she remembered that Dudley's dune buggy hadn't been beside his motor home. Maybe Pete knew that Dudley had gone and was secretly gloating about that. Fresh anger washed over her.

Mr. Logan, the English teacher, came in then, and the class came to order. Standing behind his desk, he said, "First thing this morning I want to announce a contest, with a real trophy, provided by me, to be awarded to the winner."

There was a mixture of reactions, from scoffing to groaning, and some mild enthusiasm. Betsy did not react. She wasn't certain what to expect, so she wasn't sure what her own feelings would be.

Mr. Logan explained the contest. Each person in the class was to write a composition on some phase of history, preferably something related to the local area. "Mrs. Nesbit will help judge," he said. "And there will be two runners-up, but only one trophy, for the best report." The top three reports would be read in class, and the trophy presented then.

From the back of the room, someone quipped, "At least one of us will become famous."

Mr. Logan grinned. "But never fear, each and every report will receive a grade."

Again there were groans, which Mr. Logan cheerfully ignored as he explained that the compositions would be due before the Thanksgiving holidays. "Except for the limitation that the composition must be about the history of something, preferably local, I'll leave the subject matter up to you," he told them.

Betsy glanced at Pete Davis and saw the gleam of interest in his eyes. It wasn't hard to guess that Pete's subject would be Indian picture writing.

But what could she write about? She was too new to the desert, and she felt almost as if it were her enemy. How could she work up enough enthusiasm about any part of the area's history to make an interesting composition?

But she had always been a good student, and she knew that somehow she would have to come up with something acceptable. For a few minutes she allowed herself to daydream. She imagined herself writing such a tremendous composition that she was awarded the trophy for the best one. She even saw in her mind's eye the rapt attention paid by the class as her composition was read. That was one way, she thought, that she could win the attention and respect of the other kids at Desertview High, by writing the composition that would win the trophy. At the same time, she could prove to the triad girls that she didn't live in a dump.

Mr. Logan had gone on to today's assignment now. With his back turned to the class, he was writing dates on the chalkboard.

Betsy was not paying attention to what he was writing. Instead, she was thinking about the paper she must write. And the more she thought about it, the more determined she became to put everything she had into her composition. There was one phase of local history that she was closer to than any other. Mrs. Nesbit had said she lived right on top of the old stagecoach route. She would go to the library and get all the material she could find on the Butterfield Stage. Surely she could write an interesting paper on something that lay right at her feet.

Only a small shadow of doubt crept in to dim the shining glow of Betsy's daydream about being awarded the trophy for the best composition. That shadow took the form of Pete Davis. Pete was so deeply interested in the Indian picture writing that he was certain to turn in a good composition. Could Betsy outdo him?

I *will!* she told herself silently. I'll dig out every scrap of material I can find on the Butterfield Stage, and I'll write the best composition, no matter how hard I have to work!

Chapter Seven

When Betsy came out of the high school that afternoon, she couldn't believe her eyes. Just as in her fantasy the night before, Dudley deShon was waiting for her. The only difference was that instead of driving his red Porsche, he sat at the wheel of the dune buggy.

The triad, Tina, Margo, and Stacy, were on hand to witness her triumph as Dudley hailed her, and so was Pete Davis. The real Pete, unlike the Pete of her fantasy, stood beside Stacy, and they were holding hands. But not even that could mar Betsy's elation over the fact that Dudley had come to school to give her a ride home. Apparently he hadn't given up on her just because she panicked when he tried to kiss her.

She hurried over the sidewalk until she came up to the dune buggy. "Hi," she said. "I thought maybe you'd gone away." As soon as the words were out, she wished she hadn't said them. She hadn't wanted him to think that she had worried about his absence or even noticed it.

"Who, me?" He grinned. "No way. I was only scouting around for something interesting to do. And I found it. Down in Mexico. Hop in and we'll run down to Mexicali so that I can show you around."

"Now?" she said.

"Sure. School's out. Why not?"

She hesitated. "Well, for one thing, I rode my bike to school. I can't leave it here all night."

"Not to worry. We'll just dump it in the back of this tub and drop it off at the campground."

"Anyway, I have to make sure it's okay with my parents if I'm going so far away."

He turned to frown at her. "You still insist on getting parental permission for dates?"

Betsy felt heat rush to her face. "Well, not ordinarily, of course not. But . . .well, after all, we'll be going into another country and—"

"And they might think I was taking you across the border for immoral purposes?" His mouth had twisted with scorn.

"Oh, no, not that, silly." She tried for a light laugh, but his words had made her think. Maybe that was what her parents might assume. "They trust me!" she said, defensiveness sharpening her voice. Then, when she realized how that might sound, she added, "And they like you a lot, so I'm sure they trust you, too."

"Well, they'd better, because they're going to see a lot of me from now on. Come on, doll, get your bike and let's go."

Now it was a warm glow that spread over Betsy as she hurried to the bike rack, unlocked her bicycle and brought it back to the dune buggy. Out of the corner of her eye she saw that the three girls, and Pete, were still standing in a cluster beneath a palm tree. They were trying to appear nonchalant, but Betsy noticed their occasional surreptitious glances as they observed what she and Dudley were doing.

She felt warmly triumphant as they drove away from the curb.

As they sped along the road, Dudley said, "Who were those girls in the audience?"

"What audience?"

"The ones standing over by the palm tree eyeing us. Friends of yours? The girls, I mean."

Betsy made a face. "More like my enemies. Mr.

Logan calls them the triad. They're always together and they do everything alike."

"Including making out with your boyfriend?"

"I don't have a boyfriend," she said, then silently added, although I'd like to think you are mine now.

He dismissed Pete with a shrug. "Those girls in your class?"

"Yes, especially English." She began to tell him about the composition Mr. Logan had assigned. "It has to be something about the desert, and that's not going to be easy because I hate the desert."

"Can't blame you," he said.

He switched the conversation around to talk about the excitement he expected to find in Mexicali.

She should have known that someone as old and sophisticated as Dudley deShon would be bored by high school gossip. She spent the remainder of the ride listening to him and asking questions she hoped sounded intelligent.

When they reached the house, Betsy saw that her mother was not sitting as usual in the sunshine on the patio. Fear stabbed at her. Had she suffered a relapse? As soon as Dudley brought the dune buggy to a halt, she sprang out and ran toward the house. Opening the screen door, she called, "Mom! Oh, Mom, are you okay?"

"Of course I'm all right, Betsy." Her mother's voice rang with a new note of excitement. "I'm here in the kitchen, dear. Come see what I've found."

Betsy ran through the house and stopped at the kitchen doorway. Her mother sat on a high stool at the counter, the top of which was covered now with newspapers. Dirty rags were strewn across the newspapers and a big jar of brass polish stood open. Mrs. Alexander held up a small bell of gleaming brass. Although its handle was missing, Betsy recognized it as an old-fashioned school bell, like the one she had seen in a book about a country schoolteacher of long ago.

"Doesn't it have a lovely tone?" Mrs. Alexander

said as she gave the bell a little shake. The note sounded clear and beautiful. "Just as beautiful as the day it was cast," she said.

"Hey, lady, what have you been up to?"

Betsy had almost forgotten about Dudley until she heard his voice from directly behind her. She stepped into the kitchen, and Dudley followed her to cross to where Mrs. Alexander sat. She held out the bell to him, and he took it and rang it again. "Not bad for an old piece of junk," he said.

Betsy's mother laughed, the most carefree sound Betsy had heard from her since her illness. "Junk is what it was about to become, if I hadn't rescued it." She explained that she had taken her campstool out this morning to the old adobe ruin. "While I enjoyed the desert's sunlight, I sifted through some of that pile of dirt. I came up with this, but it wasn't until I'd worked on it for hours that it got back its lovely gleam."

"It's really nice," Betsy said and meant it. She was happy that her mother had found some interest here in the desert. "But Dudley and I are in sort of a hurry. We're on our way to Mexicali. You don't mind if I go with him today, do you, Mom?"

"Down into Mexico, Betsy?" The doubtful frown that creased her mother's forehead sent Betsy's heart diving to her toes.

"Mexicali is just barely across the border, Mom. It isn't like going to Acapulco or Mexico City or like that."

"I should hope not," her mother said. "No, Betsy, I'm sorry, but I would worry about you crossing the border." She turned to Dudley and said, "You see, we're from the Middle West where you really have to go a great distance to cross a border. We're not used to running back and forth from one country to another. You understand, don't you?"

"Sure. I understand. You want to keep an eye on this beautiful daughter. And I know Betsy wants to help you hunt for treasure in that ruin. I could tell by the way she jumped out of the dune buggy and raced into the house."

"But that wasn't—" Betsy began to protest. "I didn't even know—"

"It's okay, sweetheart. Don't feel you have to apologize. I'll find something exciting to do, even though you're not with me. Be seeing you." With a casual wave of his hand, Dudley swung around and walked out of the house.

Betsy hurried after him, but already he had leaped into the dune buggy, and the whir of its starter blocked out her call to him. "Wait!" she cried. "I didn't mean—" But she was calling uselessly to the quickly disappearing back of the vehicle, and Dudley didn't even turn around to see her wave.

With a great sigh, Betsy let her shoulders droop as she turned around and reentered the house. Before she could escape to her room to be alone, her mother met her in the living room as she came in. "Wasn't that nice of Dudley to be so understanding," Mrs. Alexander said.

"Understanding!" Betsy couldn't keep the irritation from her voice. "He was just glad to get rid of me, once he found you wouldn't trust me to go to Mexico with him!"

"Oh, Betsy, it isn't that I don't trust you. Dudley knows that."

"He does? Then why did he kid me about it when I told him I'd have to check with you guys before I could go with him?"

Her mother shook her head sorrowfully. "Betsy, dear, just because this one boy goes off without you once doesn't mean the end of the world."

"You think it doesn't, because you don't understand," Betsy wailed.

"I understand that he is too old for you, dear. You'll find life much easier if you stick to friends closer to your own age, especially boys who aren't too sophisticated for you to handle."

"I could handle Dudley all right, if you'd just let me do it my way."

The kitchen door opened and Mr. Alexander came in. He walked directly to the living room, where he stopped in the doorway. "What goes on here?" he said, his tone showing that he was at least half serious. "I could practically hear the tension crackle as soon as I opened the door."

Only now did Betsy notice the lines of strain that had replaced the happiness she had seen earlier on her mother's face. She had broken her promise to herself, to keep things moving smoothly until her mother's complete recovery was assured. She had caused those stress lines now by her own selfish behavior, being nasty just because she couldn't go to Mexicali with Dudley deShon.

"Oh, Mom, I'm sorry," she said and ran to throw her arms around her mother. "I know I shouldn't take out my disappointment on you. You had to do what you thought best."

"Well," her father said, "it would seem that peace has been restored. I'll just go out and make my grand entry again so that everybody can forget whatever caused the tension." He made a great show of doing exactly that, and in seconds he had Mrs. Alexander laughing again. Even Betsy had to smile, although her heart ached for the disappointments and frustrations that lay buried beneath the grievances she had stormed about to her mother. Her mom, she knew, would never understand the terrible adjustment she was having to make here in Shelter Valley. And now, more than ever, Betsy knew that she could not let her find out. Not ever.

She went to her room and changed into her old jeans and T-shirt, her working clothes. Dudley had said that she was eager to help her mother dig among the ruins, hoping to find interesting relics. She might as well pretend she was.

Mrs. Alexander was pleased to have Betsy working with her. Betsy even thought her mother was taking special care to make the sifting process interesting to her. And in a way it was nice to be working together. It was good to have her mom feeling well enough to participate in things again, and Betsy tried to push Dudley, the triad girls, and even Pete Davis into the far recesses of her mind.

Even in mid-afternoon the sun was warm on their heads as they worked, digging gently with old kitchen spoons and sifting through the sandy dirt with their bare hands.

"I know that archaeologists use brushes to brush away the dirt from the artifacts they find," Mrs. Alexander said. "But of course we're not true archaeologists."

"And our finds aren't as valuable," Betsy added.

"Oh, I wouldn't say that. Maybe the things we find aren't as old as those from King Tut's tomb, but the Butterfield Stage stopped running about the time of the Civil War, so the things could be well over a hundred years old."

Betsy sat back on her heels and looked at her mother. "How do you know about the Butterfield Stage?"

Mrs. Alexander laughed. "Remember that time we stopped at the ranger station? While you went to the restroom I read some of their literature."

Betsy went back to work without saying anything further. Why did her mother get so excited about old, broken stuff that someone had probably tossed out long ago? Trash. The pile of ruin they were digging in now had probably been the trash heap once. Maybe the triad girls were right. Maybe this was a dump, but that was a long time ago, and it wasn't a dump now. She'd help her mother go through the stuff because she had promised herself to cooperate in her recovery, but Betsy's personal reason for working so hard on the adobe rubble was to get rid of the unsightly heap so that the triad girls could not possibly say she lived at the dump.

They found nothing more that day except some bits of broken china and part of an old picture frame. Betsy's mother became excited over the picture frame piece. There were scrolls and curlicues of some material, possibly wood, that had been covered with gold. Time and earth had dulled the gold, but that didn't lessen Mrs. Alexander's enthusiasm. "Just think, Betsy," she said. "This frame probably once held someone's treasured portrait. Or maybe a silhouette of some child." She explained that profiles cut out of darker paper and pasted on a light background were popular in the early eighteen hundreds. "Let's take that into the house and I'll clean it up so it'll shine like new."

"Okay," Betsy said. So, she thought, after it's cleaned up, what have you got? A broken piece of picture frame that isn't good for anything. Still, if it helped make her mother happy here in the desert, there was no harm in taking it back to the house.

By then the sun had sunk low on the horizon, and the air was growing cool. They went inside where her mother took a short rest before starting to prepare their evening meal.

Betsy went into her room to begin on her homework. She opened her math book, but her thoughts strayed to the composition she had to write for Mr. Logan. Thanksgiving vacation, the deadline for handing in the report, seemed a long time away, but Betsy knew that time had a way of speeding up when something like this project was due. And she hadn't the slightest idea of where or how to begin writing about the history of the Butterfield Stage.

Just as her mother called her to come help with preparing the meal, Betsy decided that she would have to go to the library after school next day and see what she could find on the subject. Probably Pete Davis had his report half finished by now. She couldn't let him get ahead of her!

Chapter Eight

Next morning at breakfast Betsy told her parents that she would be late getting home from school. "I have to find out something about the Butterfield Stage so that I can begin my theme. Maybe the library will have something."

"I'll be interested in whatever you find," her mother said. "I'm becoming a real history buff, at least where that stagecoach run is concerned. It fascinates me."

Betsy thought her mother should be the one who had to write the theme. Already she was sick of the project. If it hadn't been for her determination to win Mr. Logan's trophy and with it the admiration of the class, she would have been tempted to scrap the whole thing. But then there was her own pride. She had never goofed off an assignment yet and she didn't intend to start now.

In math class that day, Kathy Jenkins, who sat in front of Betsy and had been absent the day before, did not understand the assignment.

Mr. Dangerfield asked Betsy to explain the material they had covered. "You seemed to have a good grasp of those formulas and how to use them, Betsy, so why don't the two of you take your work to the back of the room and work at the table while the rest of us do a few warming-up exercises with our brains."

Mr. Dangerfield really went for what he called warming-up exercises. The kids knew they were mini tests, but he wouldn't admit that. In any case, Betsy was glad to escape today's.

While they were working, Kathy said, "You know, Betsy, I really like you. I've wanted to be friendly, but, well—" She shrugged her shoulders. "You know."

Betsy did know. She pressed her lips together and sighed. "But you can't because you think I live in a dump."

"Oh, no. I don't think so, but, well— Really." She gave a nervous little laugh.

"But Margo Graham and Tina Hatfield and Stacy Carlat *say* I live in a dump. That's it, isn't it, Kathy?"

Kathy ducked her head so that her long blond hair that was parted in the center the way the triad girls wore theirs fell over her face like a curtain shutting her off from Betsy. Kathy was pretty, but Betsy realized all of a sudden that she had no individuality. She looked like an imitation of the other girls, and Betsy knew that an imitation was never as good as the original.

"Kathy, why don't you do your own thinking instead of letting those girls do it for you?" she asked.

"But, Betsy, you don't understand. Here at Desertview High, if Stacy and Margo and Tina chop you down, you're gone! Oh, what a jerk I am!" Her hand flew to cover her mouth, and as she looked up at Betsy her eyes were wide with distress. "I had to go and talk when— Well, what I meant was that I just couldn't hack it if they ran me down the way they have you." Her blue eyes apologized for the frank admission.

"Don't worry, Kathy," Betsy said. "I know what they say about me, but I've just decided to forget it. I'm going to do my own thing. I'm going to dress the way I want to and not try to be like them or to please them. From now on I'm going to be *me* and nobody else."

Kathy sighed. "I really admire you, Betsy. Really. I

wish I could be as strong as you are, but I just can't afford to strike out on my own. I need their support."

"Well, I think you're doing yourself an injustice, Kathy. But if that's the way you feel, we'd better get back to math. Somebody might notice that we're getting friendly and cut off your life support system." Betsy knew that there was a little cruelty in her saying that, but she couldn't help being hurt that her one possible friend in Desertview High didn't have the guts to stand up for the friendship.

At least, she thought, this talk with Kathy had strengthened her determination to stop being a sheep.

After school that day Betsy spent two hours in the library searching for material on the Butterfield Stage. With the librarian's help she found out a few facts, but that was all they were—facts. Like, the Butterfield Stage route followed a trail made by Kit Carson and General Kearny's Army of the West. Later, Colonel St. George Cooke and his Mormon Battalion blazed the first wagon road into Southern California in 1847, following this same trail. Still later it became the Southern Emigrant Trail and then in 1857 the first stagecoach carried mail across it.

Facts, cold, dull facts, Betsy thought as she reread the notes she had taken. The desert's history was as dry as its sandy soil.

She had done all she could for today. She slammed the book closed. Even the faint odor that drifted up to her nostrils from the book with her gesture was stale, old, dull. She returned the book to the shelf, gathered up her own books and her jacket and left the library, pedaling home on her bike.

When she came onto the patio her mother was lying on the chaise in the still-warm sunlight. "Hello, dear," she said. "I hope your work at the library was satisfactory, because you missed some charming visitors."

"Oh?" Betsy's thoughts whirled through the limited possibilities. Her mom couldn't have meant Dudley, because she'd hardly call him a visitor since he was staying in the campground. Could it have been Pete Davis? But she had said visitors, so there must have been more than one. "Who was it?" she asked.

"Some girls from your school. They were so interested in our campground. Your father took them all through it, and he said they wanted to know all about the occupants of each campsite. Then they stopped back here and visited with me for quite a while. I served them the rest of that lemonade you made. I was sure you'd want me to offer it to them."

The more her mother talked about the girls, the more surprised Betsy became. She thought she could guess who they were, but she couldn't think why they should show this sudden burst of interest in the campground they had dubbed the dump. "Were there three of them?" she asked.

"Yes. Charming girls. Their names are Stacy, Margo and Tina. It was Stacy who was driving, and she seemed to be the one who was most interested. I think she knows Dudley. She was curious about his motor home. I guess none of them had seen one as big as that."

"Did Dudley join you?" Betsy couldn't help asking.

"Oh, no. He wasn't here. I urged the girls to come back sometime when you were here. They said they know you."

"Yes," Betsy said. "I know them."

"I'm glad you're making friends here in Shelter Valley, dear. You'll be much happier and feel more at home."

If those girls were friends, Betsy thought, she'd as soon have enemies. But she didn't say this to her mother, who wouldn't understand. Instead, she said, "Well, I'd better go change so I can help Dad. I've goofed off enough lately." She hurried to her room.

While she was changing into her old work clothes,

NEVER SAY NEVER

her thoughts were busy. Apparently the triad girls had put on a good show of charm that had worked with her mother. Totally. Now, any criticism Betsy made of them would be called just pure bad temper.

But Betsy knew exactly why the girls had swarmed all over Sagebrush RV Park. It wasn't the campground that fascinated them, but Dudley deShon. They had seen him, and they liked what they saw. More than that, they wanted him. It wouldn't take much homework to find out that Dudley was staying at the campground, and now they were after him. Or, at least Stacy Carlat was after him. Wasn't it enough that she had Pete Davis under her thumb? Why did she have to add Dudley to her string of scalps?

"Oh, glug," Betsy muttered aloud. Scalps indeed! Now she was even using metaphors straight out of western history. How corny could you get! This desert was the pits, and she was in danger of becoming part of it! Something would have to be done about that, but right now Betsy couldn't think what.

The next day at school, to Betsy's surprise, Pete Davis joined her for lunch. Betsy had brought her own sack lunch, and she was sitting at a small table in the courtyard behind the school building. Each table was shaded by a latticed roof over which desert grasses had been spread. It was pleasantly warm here, yet shaded from the sun's glare. Because Betsy had no real friends to join her for lunch, she always brought along a book to read while she ate.

Today she was reading a romance novel. Even though she had no boyfriend, she enjoyed pretending to be involved in the romance just as the heroine of her story was.

"Is this seat taken?" Pete asked. Betsy didn't look up or answer. She couldn't believe anyone would be speaking to her, so she did not emerge from the world of the novel.

Then Pete said, "If that's local history you're so absorbed in, I can see the competition for Mr. Logan's trophy is going to be plenty stiff. Really.'' With that remark, and without waiting for her permission, he sat down opposite her and began to spread out his own lunch on the table.

At last Betsy looked up. She laughed self-consciously as she closed her book and hid it in her lap under the table. "Actually I was reading fiction. I'm afraid the local history doesn't turn me on all that much."

Pete's eyebrows shot up. "I didn't figure you for a quitter."

"I'm not," Betsy said in quick self-defense. "Don't worry, I'll get going on the composition, and I promise you plenty of competition. I just have to find the right approach. Right now the desert's history seems dry as dust to me."

Pete grinned. "That's because you haven't come up against the people who made it."

Betsy drew the corners of her mouth down. "They're all long gone. I didn't know them."

As Pete argued, his enthusiasm grew and he gestured with his half-eaten apple. "But they left their mark. Turn around and look behind you at that saddle between those two peaks back there. What do you see?"

Betsy swung around. "You mean where the skyline dips down like there might be a canyon?"

"Yeah, that's Foot and Walker Pass. The Mormon Battalion had to hack out a passage wide enough to move through. They had to use axes because they had lost their heavy digging tools on the trek west. Later, the Butterfield Stage used the same pass and named it Foot and Walker Pass."

"Why that name?" Betsy felt sure that Pete had intended for her to ask that very question, his answer was so quick.

"Because it was so steep the passengers had to get out so the horses could pull the coach up. The driver probably said, 'Okay, you guys, get out on foot and walk 'er.'"

Betsy laughed. "I think you mixed up their language and ours today, didn't you?"

Pete shrugged. "Maybe, but they had their own slang. Remember, they were real people, just like us."

Betsy sighed. "I guess so, but I can't write a whole theme about the passengers on the stagecoach getting out and pushing the coach up the hill, can I?"

"What do you want anyway, me to write your whole theme for you? Do your own research. I've got my own paper to write."

His freckles seemed to stand out even more than usual. Pete was angry. But then, so was she. She was having a hard enough time trying to work up enthusiasm for the desert without his chopping her down that way.

"Don't worry," she said. "I can do my own research. And I'd better get busy on it right now, if you'll excuse me." She stood up, gathered her lunch scraps and took them over to the trash barrel. When she glanced back, Pete had already gone. He had left without even saying good-bye.

There wasn't time, actually, for her to go to the library before her next class, so Betsy went directly to her locker to pick up the books she would need this afternoon. Her feet seemed to drag now, and her thoughts were heavy with gloom. She had really blown it with Pete now. But the blame wasn't all hers, for Pete's attitude had been pretty grungy, too.

On the other hand, her conscience reminded her, Pete had tried to help her, telling her about the pass with the quaint name. "But what good does one mangy piece of information do?" she whispered to herself. Oh, why did fate have to send her family to this dismal place anyway!

That afternoon when Betsy came home from school, her mother said, "I've half-promised you for a job, one that'll make you some spending money, if you want it."

Betsy thought of her dwindling savings. Since they came here she hadn't had much opportunity to earn money. She had been quick to agree that until the family could catch up from the recent financial drain there would be no increase in her allowance even though she spent every spare minute helping to fix up the place. That was part of the family code. They helped each other. So she really needed the money from outside jobs. "What's the deal?" she asked.

"I thought you'd be interested. The Caldwells, that family in campsite three, would like for you to baby-sit Saturday if you're free. It's Mr. and Mrs. Caldwell's wedding anniversary, and they would like to run down to Mexicali for the day."

"The family with four kids?"

"They said they'd pay double the usual fee since there are so many small ones."

"Saturday. All day?"

"Yes," her mother said. "Did you have other plans?"

"No." She didn't have plans. Not really. But she hadn't seen Dudley since she had had to turn down his invitation to go to Mexicali with him, and she had been working on a plan to offer something fun for them to do together, like maybe a picnic or something.

"This baby-sitting job might get you others so you could earn money," her mother said. "Lots of people who camp have children, and if word gets around that there is a built-in baby-sitter here at Sagebrush, it might help the campground as well as being a source of income for you, Betsy."

What her mother said was true. Anyway, how did she know that Dudley would like the idea of a picnic? He'd probably think that was pure corn. She tried to smile. "Okay, Mom. You can tell them the deal is on."

Mrs. Alexander's smile was warm as she looked up

NEVER SAY NEVER 77

at Betsy. "Why don't you run down there now and tell Mrs. Caldwell yourself, dear. That way you could make arrangements and settle on the fee. Besides, I'm so comfortable here in the sunshine that I don't want to move."

"Oh, sure, Mom. You stay there and soak up the sun. I'll leave my books here and run down now before I change."

Mrs. Caldwell was a pleasant-faced, plump woman, and her children seemed well behaved and happy as they gathered around Betsy, clamoring to know if she was their new baby-sitter. She thought that at least it would be a change from working on the campground, which she would probably be doing all day Saturday otherwise.

They set the time for her arrival, and the fee was more than ample, so when Betsy returned to her house she found that she was almost looking forward to Saturday.

But when Friday afternoon came, she wished she had not made the arrangements to baby-sit next day. To her surprise, when she came out of the school building, Dudley was waiting for her. "Stow your bike and I'll take you to the Pizza House for a snack, Betsy," he said and leaped over the side of the dune buggy to hoist the bike into the rear of the vehicle.

Betsy was too thrilled to notice that he had commanded instead of inviting her to go with him. "Hey, I thought you'd forgotten all about me," she said.

He grinned at her, shaking his head until his dark hair swung around his ears. "You're too much of a challenge to forget. I've got to help you grow up, bring you up to my level. Come on. Let's get moving."

Betsy climbed into the passenger's seat and they started off with a roar of the motor. This time, to Betsy's disappointment, neither Pete nor the triad girls stood by to see her triumph.

The Pizza House was one of the favorite hangouts of the high school crowd, but today very few were there that Betsy recognized. Again she was disappointed that no one she knew had seen her with the exciting Dudley.

She said she wanted only part of a pizza, and suggested that they order one and divide it. But Dudley would not listen to such a suggestion. "Nothing but the best for my girl," he said and ordered a large pizza with everything Betsy could think of on it for her and another for himself.

"I'll never be able to eat all that," she protested.

Dudley shrugged. "Not to worry. Their garbage cans are probably hungry anyway."

"But it's a waste of—"

He reached across and laid his hand over her mouth. "Those words are a no-no. Remember deShon Plastics."

Betsy persisted, "Surely even deShon Plastics's money must have a limit somewhere, and if you keep on—"

"If it has a limit, I haven't found it yet, and I've been giving it my best efforts for years," he said with a laugh. Then he quickly changed the subject. "I've got plans for us tomorrow, sweetheart."

"Tomorrow?" Betsy's breath caught in her throat. "That's Saturday."

Apparently he didn't notice her distress, for he said, "Sure it's Saturday. Like, no school. You're free as air, and there's a fiesta in Borrego Springs. You know, square dancing in the streets, all that. It's just corny enough that it might be a laugh. We'll spend as much time as we want there and then—"

She couldn't let him go on. Interrupting, she said, "Dudley, I can't." Her voice came out a wail. "I'm sorry. I'd really love to go with you, but I have to baby-sit."

"So, break the date. Tell 'em you have other plans you forgot about."

Betsy shook her head. "They're counting on me, Dudley."

"So tell 'em you sprained your ankle, you broke

your back, you have smallpox and you might give it to the kids. Tell 'em anything."

Betsy sat up straighter and tilted her chin. "I can't do that. It would be a lie."

"So what's a little lie if it gets you what you want?"

"Dudley, I don't operate that way."

"Then you're missing a lot in life."

"Maybe so, but at least I can live with my conscience."

"Doll, I wouldn't have your conscience if you gave it to me. Come on, let's split. This place is dull city."

"But you haven't finished your pizza, and I've only—"

"Forget it." Already he was on his feet, striding toward the door.

Betsy slid out of the booth and hurried after him.

They rode back to the campground in silence. Betsy was hunched down in the bucket seat, thinking dark thoughts. Why couldn't Dudley see things her way just once? At times like these she almost hated him. But then she reminded herself that he was older, and if she wanted the thrill of being known as Dudley deShon's girl, she would just have to put up with the differences in their approaches to life. But now, she thought in glum silence, I've probably even squashed my last chance of being known as Dudley's girl.

Chapter Nine

On Saturday morning Betsy went to her baby-sitting job with less enthusiasm than she might have had if she hadn't been forced to turn down another invitation from Dudley deShon.

But Mr. and Mrs. Caldwell's excitement over their anniversary outing cheered her a little. At least she was contributing to someone else's happiness. And the children were excited about the prospect of being entertained by a new young person.

"They'll give you a good break when they take their afternoon nap," Mrs. Caldwell said. "They play so hard all morning that by afternoon they're ready to sleep for several hours, especially since it's dark inside our tent."

"I'm sure we'll get along fine, Mrs. Caldwell," Betsy said. "Don't worry about a thing. My parents are here in case of any emergency, but I don't expect to have to call on them."

"I know you're a dependable girl," Mrs. Caldwell said. "I'm a good judge of people."

Mr. Caldwell was urging her to come on so they wouldn't waste a minute of their free day, so with a hug and kiss for each of her children, she hurried out to their car.

As the car disappeared around a curve in the driveway, with all of them waving still, the youngest child, Timmie, turned a solemn face to Betsy and said, "My mommie and daddy will come back, won't they, Betsy?"

Betsy caught him up in her arms and hugged him. "Of course they'll come back, Timmie. They wouldn't want to be without a sweet little guy like you for very long. They'd miss you too much."

Timmie seemed to be reassured by her words, but Betsy made a special effort after that to see that the children were well entertained so there would be no time for insecure feelings and doubts. She helped them build a city in the sandy dirt, with wide streets on which they could run their miniature cars. When this game threatened to turn into a disaster with too many car wrecks, she found one of their storybooks, and taking Timmie on her lap, read to them until they began to grow restless.

She took them on a walk around the campground where they searched for interesting sights. They watched a lizard doing push-ups on a sunny rock. This was when Betsy had to do some fast talking in order to convice the oldest, Andy, that lizards didn't like to be caught any more than he would like for some giant to grab him and squeeze him in his hand. Timmie seemed to have forgotten his uneasiness about his parents leaving. She even took them to the small playground inside the RV park, where they spent another half-hour.

After the strenuous morning, Betsy was glad when noon came. She looked forward to the respite she would have during their naptime.

She heated soup on the portable propane stove Mr. Caldwell had shown her how to work, and unwrapped the sandwiches that Mrs. Caldwell had left in the ice chest for her to serve with the apples and milk.

Timmie's eyes had become so heavy that she saw it was hard for him to keep them open long enough to finish his lunch. She took him into the tent and put him down first for his nap. The others were ready almost as soon. At last all had been tucked into their sleeping bags and peace stole over the campground. All the other campers had gone for the day, probably to the fiesta that Dudley had wanted to take her to.

Betsy settled herself in the lacy shade of a thorn tree, facing the tent where she had left the door flap unzipped with the sides spread back so that she could see if any of the children stirred inside the tent. Meanwhile, she would read.

She had barely started a chapter when she heard a car approach on the gravel drive. Wondering who it might be, she turned her head and recognized her own family's car. Her mother was driving, and to Betsy's surprise, her father sat in the passenger's seat.

The car pulled to a stop beside her and her mother leaned out the window and said, "Everything okay, Betsy?"

"Sure, Mom, but what's up with you two?"

"Your father got a cactus thorn embedded in the palm of his hand, and the more I tried to get it out, the deeper it buried itself. It must be a barbed thorn. Anyway, we're going to run into town to the hospital's emergency room and have them get it out."

"Ugh!" Betsy shivered. "How awful for you, Dad."

"Oh, I think I'll live," he kidded. "But my hand isn't good for much with the extra finger this thorn gives it. Think you can hold down the fort until we get back?"

"No problem," Betsy said. "These kids ought to be out for a couple of hours, the way they ran all morning."

"You're ready for a little rest yourself, huh?"

"You can say that again. They're four dynamos."

"We shouldn't be gone long," Mrs. Alexander said. "I'm sure this will be just a routine job in that emergency room, but I don't have the equipment or the know-how."

"Take your time, and don't worry about us," Betsy assured them, and with a wave they drove away.

Quiet settled over the desert. It was like no quiet Betsy had ever known. Every slight sound was magnified by the vast silence of the desert. High overhead a jet plane made a faint rumble like the most distant thunder. Betsy craned her neck to see the plane. At first she couldn't find any trace of it, but when she scanned the entire sky she discovered the white vapor trail far from where she had expected it by the sound. After the sound faded away the silence returned, complete and enveloping. A little later, the hum that she thought must be a helicopter turned out to be no more than a bee drifting lazily from dry weed to creosote bush.

The sun was so bright, the sky such an intense blue, and the slender stalks of dry grass waving gently in the light breeze all added up to make a hypnotic effect. When Betsy turned her attention to her book, the words swam together on the printed page, and her eyelids felt as if they were being drawn together.

The romance novel no longer held her interest. Instead, her thoughts strayed to Dudley deShon and the fiesta in Borrego Springs. What if she had gone with him? What would they be doing now? She pictured herself and Dudley joining the throngs of people dancing in the streets to the strains of a mariachi band. That would be a really romantic setting. Maybe Dudley would try to kiss her again. This time she would let him. Maybe she'd even respond. She smiled at the lovely picture in her thoughts.

She was so engrossed in those thoughts that she did not hear the crunch of gravel under tires as the dune buggy approached. When Dudley leaped out and came to stand over her, Betsy thought for an instant that it was just part of her daydream, her fantasy.

"Aren't you even going to say hi?" he asked.

Betsy sprang to her feet so quickly that for an instant she was dizzy and had to close her eyes. Dudley was quick to put his arm around her.

"You okay?" he said.

"Yes." Suddenly she was okay as she realized that it was the real Dudley standing beside her, no longer just her fantasy. "I—I just didn't expect you, that's all."

He chuckled. "That's the way to go. Surprise 'em. Knock 'em cold. That's what I like to do."

"I thought you went to Borrego Springs."

"Agh, when you wouldn't go with me I sort of hung around looking for some action. Before I found any, I saw your parents drive away." He gave her a sly wink. "Thought I'd come back and see if we couldn't stir up some here. What'd you do with the brats?"

A small feeling of uneasiness began to creep along Betsy's spine. She wanted to be with Dudley, and yet . . . "They're down for naps," she said. "But the Caldwell children aren't brats, not really. They're just full of energy."

He shrugged. "Well, whatever. Anyway, they're asleep, your folks are gone, nobody's watching. Why don't we go for a spin in the dune buggy?"

"Go off and leave the kids alone? No way, Dudley."

"Who's to know? I'll have you back before they wake up."

"That's not what a good baby-sitter does."

"Like I said, who's to know? You'll get paid just the same."

Still Betsy shook her head. "The money isn't everything."

"No?" He laughed. "That's not what you've been telling me."

"The Caldwells trust me."

"Oh, Betsy, when are you going to learn that the world isn't full of set rules: good is good and bad is bad."

A sudden wave of anger washed over Betsy. She had her own code, and she wasn't about to let him change it even to give her a stolen hour or two in his company. "I know very well that nothing is either all good or all bad, but I also know that Mr. and Mrs. Caldwell have trusted me to take the best care I can of their children until they get back, and not even you, Dudley deShon, can tempt me to do less than my best."

He caught her eyes with his own and held them as he said, without any emphasis or expression, "Okay, if that's it, that's it. See you around. Maybe." With a mock salute he sprang into his dune buggy and drove out of the campground.

What was wrong with her? Betsy wondered when the desert's quiet had settled around her again. First she had had a fight with Pete Davis, and now she'd had one with Dudley deShon. She had practically handed both of them over to Stacy Carlat. "I ought to write a book on how to make enemies," she said aloud, softly.

She felt a small tugging on the leg of her jeans and broke out of her own dismal thoughts to find that Andy was trying to get her attention.

"Betsy, hey, Betsy," he said. "Timmie's gone."

For an instant Betsy just looked at him. Then full realization of what he had said came to her, and she bent her knees to stoop down to Andy's level. "Wh . . . what did you say, Andy?"

"Timmie's not in his sleeping bag. He isn't anywhere. He's gone."

"He can't be. I was here all the time!" But instantly Betsy knew that although physically she had not left, her attention had been diverted, first by her fantasy, and then by the very real appearance of Dudley himself. During that time Timmie could have slipped out of the tent.

"Maybe he went to the toilet, you know, the bathroom in the middle of the campground," she said.

Andy shook his head. "He never goes by himself. He's afraid there's a bear inside that building."

"Oh, Andy, of course there's no bear."

"I know that!" Andy said, scoffing at the absurdity

NEVER SAY NEVER 87

in his most grown-up manner. "But Timmie's little and he—"

"Andy, we're wasting time talking. Did you see Timmie go out of the tent? Which way—" But already Andy was shaking his head solemnly.

"I just woke up and saw he was gone. I thought he was out here with you."

"He can't have gone far." Betsy hoped that was true. "We've got to find him!" But how, her mind asked without answer. "Andy, why do you think he would go out of the tent?"

"Maybe he went to find Mom and Dad."

"Oh, no!" Betsy cried. Terrible thoughts swarmed in her mind, of where such a quest might take the small boy.

If only her own parents hadn't had to go into town. She couldn't leave the other children alone while she went to search for Timmie. Yet she couldn't drag them along with her. She didn't even know where to begin looking. She thought of the warning Pete Davis had given her, about the dangers of venturing out into the desert if you didn't know where you were going. And such a little boy too! He would be frightened. Tears sprang to her eyes and she brushed them away with a gesture that was full of anger. Think, Betsy! she told herself. Think!

"Let's check the campground first, Andy. Are the others still asleep?"

He indicated that they were, and Betsy said, "Then will you run over to the bathroom and make sure Timmie isn't there? I'll wait right here, and you go straight there and come right back, don't go anywhere else, okay?"

"Okay, Betsy," he said, apparently feeling proud to be given the responsibility.

But when he came back, he shook his head. Timmie had not been in the bathroom.

Betsy decided to wake the other children and take

them with her while she searched the campground.

What if she had slipped away with Dudley as he wanted her to do? Betsy knew she would never be able to live with her conscience if she had done that! It was bad enough as it stood now. If only Dudley hadn't come and distracted her. But that wasn't entirely fair, she thought, to put all the blame on Dudley. Before he came, she had been daydreaming. Timmie could have come out of the tent during that time and she probably wouldn't have noticed him. If only she hadn't been daydreaming about Dudley!

If only, if only, if only! Betsy thought with impatience. She sighed. Life seemed to be made up of *if onlys*, but now she couldn't afford the luxury of wishful thinking. She needed all her power of thought to help her find Timmie. He must be somewhere in the campground, and they would find him if they searched thoroughly enough.

The search seemed to take forever, since Betsy had to slow her own pace to match the children's short strides. They called and shouted every few minutes along the way, but no matter how carefully they listened, there was no piping childish voice to answer and bring reassurance. In time, she had to admit that Timmie was nowhere within the limits of the campground.

If there were someone, some adult, left in the campground to help her or to advise her, she thought. But there was no one, and Betsy knew that whatever decisions were made would have to be made by her.

There was no choice. She would have to get outside help. But who? The answer came quickly. The ranger station. Pete Davis had talked about the ranger and how often he had to go out and hunt for people who got lost in the desert. Betsy decided to take the children with her to her house and phone the ranger station. Maybe the ranger would come and help find Timmie.

With the three children, she started toward the house. Susie, the girl twin, began to whimper. Without stopping, Betsy reached down and swung her up in her arms. "What's the matter, Susie?" she said.

"Won't we ever see Timmie again? Is he lost?"

Betsy caught her breath. She swallowed and braced herself as she said, making her voice firm and strong, "Of course we'll see him again. He's only a little bit lost, and we're going to phone the ranger. He'll find Timmie in no time."

Reassured, Susie snuggled down against Betsy's shoulder. "I like you, Betsy."

Tears stung Betsy's eyes, and she blinked them back. She only hoped that Susie could still say that by nightfall, because if they couldn't find Timmie by then— She dared not think beyond that.

Chapter Ten

Inside the house she found the ranger station's number and dialed it, then held her breath for fear there might not be an answer.

She heard the buzz as the phone rang three times. She was trembling all over when at last it was answered.

"Ranger station, Pete Davis speaking."

Betsy was thrown completely off balance. "Pete! What? How? I dialed the ranger station," she exclaimed.

"This is the ranger station. May I help you?" Maybe he didn't recognize her voice.

Betsy was more confused than ever. "What are you doing there?" she asked.

"I work here part time. Is this Betsy Alexander?"

Abruptly Betsy was reminded of the reason for her call. "Yes. Pete, something terrible's happened and I need the ranger's help!"

"Take it easy, Betsy. Just tell me what your problem is. I'll relay your message to the ranger if— I'll see that you get whatever help you need."

He sounded so calm that Betsy felt a little better. She explained about the missing child.

Pete didn't waste time asking questions. "We'll be right out, Betsy. Just hang in there, girl," he said.

"Don't panic. The ranger's good at finding strays lost in the desert, and I know that area pretty well too. Stay right where you are. Okay?"

"Okay. And thanks, Pete." But already he had rung off.

"Hang in there," Pete had said, just as if the two of them had not had that terrible quarrel in the courtyard at school. On the phone Pete had sounded really concerned, but at the same time confident. She couldn't help but compare his concern with the way she knew Dudley would have acted. Mrs. Nesbit had said that Pete was a responsible boy, and now he had shown that sense of responsibility. Although Pete had downplayed the compliment, right now Betsy thought that a sense of responsibility was just about the best characteristic a person could have.

But Pete had also told her to stay right where she was until the ranger came. In other words, she was to do nothing about finding Timmie while she waited. How could she possibly sit here just waiting? The children were as restless as she was. Betsy longed for a good television program to distract all of them. But in this remote area with so few towns and those widely scattered, cable television was all that was available, and at this hour of the day there was nothing on. Another point against the dismal desert!

She took the children to her room and showed them her doll collection. But her dolls were the kind meant for display, not for cuddling. They had come from different foreign countries and wore typical native costumes. These children were too young to appreciate this kind of doll.

She gave them each a cookie from the cookie jar and poured small glasses of milk. She hoped this snack wouldn't spoil their supper, but at least it distracted them and gave all of them something to do to fill the long minutes of waiting.

When at last the crunch of gravel under tires announced the arrival of the ranger's green pickup truck,

Betsy breathed a great sigh of relief. At least now she would have someone to share her worry about Timmie.

Pete came with the ranger. Although Betsy might have expected this, she had during her long and agonizing wait pushed the thought to the back of her mind while she built up a defense against Pete that she hoped would banish the terrible sense of guilt she felt about Timmie's getting lost. Since Pete had warned her of the dangers of the desert, when she saw him now he would probably give her a stern lecture about how easy it is to get lost here. He'd chop her down for neglecting to watch Timmie.

What could she say in her own defense? If she admitted that she had been chatting with Dudley de-Shon, Pete would probably sneer. Why should he believe that she and Dudley had been arguing about her refusal to leave the children and go for a ride with him? Pete would probably think she had really slipped away with Dudley.

As the two approached her, Betsy could hardly keep herself from taking a step backward from them, or from putting up her arm to ward off a blow.

But it wasn't Pete who spoke first, it was the ranger, and his words were calm, reassuring. A pleasant-looking man with brown hair and a square chin, he introduced himself as Guy Olson. Then he wasted no time but asked Timmie's age. When Betsy said he was only two-and-a-half, the ranger smiled. "Then he can't have gone far," he said. "Those little legs have their limitations."

"He isn't anywhere in the campground," Betsy said. "We looked everywhere before we phoned you."

"Good girl. You've a level head on your shoulders."

His praise lifted some of the weight from Betsy's heart, although she still felt a terrible guilt.

While the ranger asked questions about what Timmie wore and anything Betsy might remember that would give them a clue, Pete had gone to the Caldwell tent to check for evidence. When Betsy and the ranger, with the children, joined him, he said, "I found a small footprint over there near the edge of the campground. It's about the size to fit the smallest shoe I found inside the tent."

Betsy gasped. "I took off his shoes when I put him down for his nap. He would have on his socks but no shoes. Oh, his poor little feet on these stones!" She was thinking also of the cactus thorn in her father's hand. What if Timmie stepped on such a thorn?

Pete and the ranger conferred for a few minutes. Betsy was not close enough to overhear their words, but she watched their gestures. They pointed one way and then another while they talked over what must be a plan.

"Maybe if you two called him, he'd hear you," she said. "The children and I tried, but our voices got swallowed up in all this open space."

The two men agreed that this was a good plan, and they cupped their hands around their mouths and called again and again, turning in different directions. But there was still no small, answering voice.

"We'd better go out," the ranger said. "Got your water canteen and your first-aid kit, Pete?"

Pete nodded. The ranger turned to Betsy. "Pete and I'll start out from different points and meet in the middle, unless one of us finds him first. We'll circle the campground, then if we don't find him we'll widen the circle on the next go-round until we do find him." He cautioned Betsy to keep the other children close beside her and to stay near the tent. "In case he should happen to find his way back," he said.

But Betsy could tell from his tone that this was as unlikely as she knew in her heart it was.

When the two had left, an overwhelming sense of loneliness swept over her. What if they couldn't find Timmie? But they had to find him! They just had to!

During the almost unendurable wait for their return,

Mr. and Mrs. Alexander returned from the hospital. When Betsy saw their car approaching along the driveway, she was so relieved that her throat closed with the overpowering desire to dissolve into tears.

When the family car drew to a stop beside Betsy and the children, only the greatest effort kept her from throwing herself into her mother's arms and bursting into tears. But she knew that for the sake of the three children still in her care she had to retain some appearance of calm.

She swallowed the lump in her throat and said, "Daddy, how is your hand? Did they get the thorn out?"

Her father held up his freshly bandaged hand. "It'll be back to normal in no time, although I must admit it's a bit awkward now." He looked a little pale. The operation must have been more than his light words made it seem.

"Isn't that the ranger's truck in the parking lot, Betsy?" her mother asked. "Everything's okay, isn't it?"

Before Betsy could break the news gently, Andy's piping voice cried, "Timmie got losted. The rangers are going to find him now."

Shock tensed her parents' faces as they turned quickly to Betsy for confirmation. She nodded. "I'm afraid that's about the way it is." She sketched in the details for them, struggling to maintain her self-control. Later she would confess about Dudley's visit, but not yet.

Already her father was opening the car door on his side. "I'll go help them search," he said.

"Now, wait a minute, darling," Mrs. Alexander said as she grabbed his arm to hold him back. "You're in no shape to go dashing around in the open desert. You'll more likely add to their problems if you pass out from weakness after what you've been through. Or at least you might get lost too, and that wouldn't help."

"You're right, I guess." He settled back in his seat.

"I'd do better to help you with Betsy and the other children. She probably needs some backup support, don't you, honey?"

Betsy made her lips smile, but she had to hide her eyes with lowered lids because the thoughtfulness made her go all soft and tearful inside.

"What will Mrs. Caldwell think of me!" she said.

Mr. Alexander said, "She'll think you're a very level-headed girl to call in the ranger while you kept the other children under supervision. Look behind you."

Betsy swung around and the sight that met her eyes turned her knees to jelly so that she could hardly stand up. Pete Davis was striding across the campground toward her, with the ranger following. Held in Pete's arms and snuggled against his shoulder was Timmie.

"Pete!" Betsy cried. "You found him!" Somehow she managed to gather together her rubbery leg muscles and run to meet him. She took Timmie from Pete's arms and hugged him, smothering him with kisses.

"Where's my mommie?" Timmie murmured sleepily.

"She'll be back pretty soon. In the meantime, I'm here and I'm going to take good care of you, Timmie. Oh, I'm so glad you're back." She turned questioning eyes toward the two rescuers. "Where— How did you find him?"

"Pete gets the credit. Tell them, Pete," the ranger said.

Pete shifted his feet and looked down at the ground, apparently embarrassed by the praise. "Well, like Guy said, he couldn't go far. It just happened that he was on my beat instead of Guy's before we met."

Timmie had become exhausted quickly, they explained, and had crawled in under an overhanging boulder and gone to sleep.

"He was dehydrated from the sun and the dry breeze, but a couple of swallows from my canteen fixed that up," Pete said. "But his feet are kind of chewed up. They'll need more attention. No thorns, just scratches." Scraggly bushes had caught his socks and pulled them off quickly, he explained. "They made clues that helped us find him."

Mr. and Mrs. Alexander joined Betsy in thanking the ranger and Pete for their help.

As Guy Olson climbed into the ranger's truck, Pete held back to speak to Betsy. When she realized his intentions, she stiffened, clutching small Timmie closer to herself. Now, she thought, here comes Pete's lecture on the dangers of the desert.

To her surprise, he said, "You really showed good thinking, Betsy, phoning for the ranger's help instead of flipping into panic, like rushing out to look for him. You'll make a good desert rat yet." He grinned and sprang into the truck as they drove away.

Desert rat, Betsy thought. She knew that term was supposed to be a compliment. Someone who knew the desert so well he was like a part of it was called a desert rat. But she didn't like being called a rat. She shuddered at the very thought. Anyway, she didn't like the desert well enough to want to become a part of it. Why couldn't Pete understand that?

Chapter Eleven

By the time Timmie's parents returned, Betsy had tenderly bathed his scratched feet and applied disinfectant, and he was able to wear his shoes again. She spent the remainder of the afternoon amusing the children with quiet activities. They had had enough excitement for one day. Too much, in fact. She told them stories and taught them some simple songs she remembered from her childhood. Determined to make up for her neglect earlier, she spent extra effort on them now.

When she had run out of other ideas for quiet games, she had all of them sit on the gravelly ground and see how many different colored pebbles they could find without moving from where they sat. Even Betsy was surprised at the variety of color and shape of the small rocks. And when they looked closely at the ground, they discovered now and then a tiny, perfect flower growing in the dry soil, no larger than the painted blossoms on the miniature design of the decorative pin someone had given her mother. Even Betsy had to admit that this was some unexpected beauty in the desert.

Timmie seemed to have forgotten all about his traumatic experience. He had even ceased worrying about when his mother would return.

But when at last their car turned into the driveway, Betsy had to grab hold of Timmie and caution the other children to wait until the car had stopped before they ran to greet their parents.

Mr. and Mrs. Caldwell had not even time to get out of the car before Andy ran to catch hold of the door handle. As the passenger's door swung open, he shouted, "Timmie ran away and got losted, but Betsy had the ranger come and find him, and he lost his socks and got his feet all scratched up so Betsy had to fix them up."

Mrs. Caldwell held up her hands. "Whoa! Slow down, Andy." She reached down and swung him up on her lap beside Timmie who had already found a place there. She turned to Timmie. "You didn't run away, Timmie! Not again! You promised!"

Timmie ducked his head while his eyes turned to look at Betsy. He nodded his head. Then, swinging around to fling his arms around his mother, he said, "You got losted. I went to find you."

"No, Timmie. I wasn't lost. Daddy and I told you we'd be back, and you see, here we are. You shouldn't have run away."

Betsy couldn't let the little boy take all the blame. "I'm afraid it was my fault, Mrs. Caldwell," she said. "I didn't watch the tent as carefully as I should have while they were sleeping."

Before she could explain further, Andy broke in to add, "I woke up and Timmie was gone."

Mr. Caldwell gave Betsy a direct look. "You're a very honest young lady," he said. "To admit that your attention lagged. We appreciate honesty."

His direct look made Betsy's stomach squirm. Did his praise carry a hint that he guessed what had distracted her? She had gone this far. She couldn't leave him speculating something that might be even worse than the truth. "I didn't leave your campsite, but I admit that for a few minutes I wasn't thinking about the children. A . . . a friend stopped by and we were talking while the children slept."

Mr. Caldwell laughed. "Your face tells me it was your boyfriend. Well, Betsy, if a girl isn't permitted a few minutes to chat with her boyfriend, the world's in a sorry state indeed. As long as Timmie was found and came to no harm, I won't criticize you." He turned to his wife. "How about you, dear?"

Mrs. Caldwell hugged Timmie again. "I agree. Betsy showed a fine sense of responsibility when she called in the ranger. And since Timmie has a history of being an escape artist, I think we owe Betsy a vote of thanks for finding him."

A great weight had been lifted from Betsy's heart. "Actually," she said, "it was Pete Davis who found Timmie." She explained that Pete worked part time in the ranger station, and how he and the ranger had worked together to find Timmie.

"I must admit that you desert young people show more levelheadedness than many of the teenagers who live in our city," Mr. Caldwell said.

Betsy opened her mouth to explain that she wasn't really a desert person and didn't intend to become one, but for some reason the words stuck in her throat and refused to come out.

The Caldwells had brought the children a *piñata*. The crepe paper animal, in the shape of a donkey, was bright pink with green ears and tail. Mrs. Caldwell explained to the children that it was stuffed with small surprise gifts, but that in order to obtain the gifts they would have to break the donkey, probably destroying it. She explained the Mexican game in which children or sometimes grown-ups at a party compete to see who can be the first to break the animal open with a stick to let the gifts fall out.

While Mr. Caldwell was paying Betsy for her hours of baby-sitting, the children were arguing because half of them wanted to break the donkey and find the gifts while the others wanted to keep the animal as it was.

Betsy slipped away, glad this was one argument she did not have to arbitrate.

Back in her own room, she recounted the money she had earned, more than she had had at one time since she left Chicago. She longed to spend it on something really special. She had worked unusually hard to earn that money, and wanted something to remind her how alert a baby-sitter must be. But in the small town of Shelter Valley, what could she find that would be special enough? With a rueful shrug of her shoulders, she carefully tucked the bills away in the secret compartment of the little oriental box in her dresser drawer, and decided to spend Sunday sifting through the old adobe ruins. At least that would be helping to reduce the size of the pile of rubble she hated so.

Sunday morning she dressed in her old working clothes and went out right after breakfast to work in the ruins. Her mother promised to join her later. "There's an article in the paper about antiques," Mrs. Alexander said. "I want to read that and the rest of the paper over a second cup of coffee. Then I have to do some hand washing, things I don't trust in the laundromat. I'll join you later."

Betsy went to the adobe ruin and sat down beside the mound of earth. For a time she looked out across the open desert. There must have been a light rain in the night because the lacy plants that grew close to the ground, dry and brown at this time of year, sparkled with tiny drops of moisture as they caught the sunlight. Off in the distance, where the desert floor dipped low to form a small, shallow bowl, a cottony puff of fog hovered just above the ground. And far in the dim distance, the mountains were silhouetted in soft gray violet. Closer at hand, in the tangle of branches of a thornbush tree, a tiny cactus wren hopped from twig to twig, its motions as quick and abrupt as if it were suspended from a coiled spring. "Are you spying on me?" She laughed as she asked the tiny, striped creature.

For a moment she gave herself up to enjoying the beauty of the desert scene. Then abruptly she said aloud, "But I don't like the desert!" Why, then, should she think it was beautiful right now?

With determination she turned her attention to digging in the heap of adobe, forcing herself to be careful in case there might be something that her mother would consider of value.

She had been working for most of an hour when, to her surprise, Dudley deShon sauntered up to talk to her. "Hey," he said, "your name isn't Mary Ann, is it?"

"Of course not! What made you say that?"

Instead of replying, he began to hum. Suddenly Betsy recognized the tune. The words told about a girl named Mary Ann who did nothing but sift sand all day. Betsy laughed.

"I guess I do look dumb sitting here digging, but I'll do almost anything to help get rid of this mess." With her hand she made a sweeping gesture to include the whole ruin.

He shook his head and made a clicking sound with his tongue. "Like I said, you're too serious. You ought to take a day off now and then. Like yesterday, you should have come with us to the fiesta. It was the greatest."

"You found someone else when I couldn't go?" Even saying the words sent a knife thrust through her chest.

"Well, naturally." He grinned.

I won't ask who it was, Betsy thought, but her tongue refused to obey the command. "Who'd you take?" she said.

"Aha, don't you wish you knew? I sense the green-eyed monster's presence."

"I'm not jealous, I was just interested," Betsy said,

and giving vent to the anger that was building up in her, she jabbed her spoon into the powdery adobe.

The spoon struck something hard, and in that instant Betsy forgot about the fiesta and jealousy, and even almost about Dudley deShon standing by her side. All her attention focused on whatever lay hidden in the adobe dust.

With great care she scraped away some of the adobe and saw a gleam as if there were something shiny buried there. It must be a large object, she thought, for she couldn't get her spoon completely under it.

Almost against her will she felt a small thrill of excitement. What if she should find something really important to history? Before the excitement died down she said, "Dudley, help me get this thing out. It might be something really good."

"Me? Dig in the dirt? You've got to have sand in your brain. I wouldn't dig in the ground if there was gold under all that trash."

"It's not trash." Betsy bit her lip. She hadn't meant to defend this mound that was the cause of her being ridiculed for living in a dump. "Well, there might be something to give us a couple of laughs. Who knows?"

"If it's laughs you want, I can find better ones for you," Dudley said. "Come on, sweetheart, this place is a drag. Let's split." He reached out to catch her hand, apparently intending to pull her to her feet to go with him.

But the sound of a horn honking caught his attention, as a car drove into the campground, and, pausing only briefly, headed straight back to where Dudley stood beside Betsy.

"Hey," he said. "Look who's here!"

He waved, and the car pulled up beside Dudley. The driver, Betsy saw, was Stacy Carlat, and with her were Margo and Tina.

"Hi," Stacy said as the three girls got out of the car. "You two digging for artifacts?" She spoke to both of them, but she was looking only at Dudley.

Betsy couldn't help herself. "How did you know about the digging?" she asked.

Stacy's smile as she turned to Betsy simpered. "Your mom can hardly talk about anything else," she said. "We stopped by the other day."

"Yeah?" Dudley broke in. "Too bad I wasn't here."

"Well, we're here again now and so are you, so what're you going to do about it?"

"I'm going to get in with you and we'll all go over to Borrego Springs and see what excitement we can stir up in that town. Come on, Betsy."

"There isn't room for Betsy," Stacy said.

"Sure there is, baby. She can sit on my lap."

"You've got to be kidding," Stacy said. "No way am I going to watch you make out with anybody but me. Not even Tina or Margo."

Dudley grinned. "Okay, then you can sit on my lap."

Betsy had had enough. She wouldn't go where she was so obviously unwanted. "Save your arguments, you guys," she said. "I'm not going anywhere. I want to see what this brass thing is I've started to uncover."

Stacy giggled. "Like mother, like daughter. A couple of dusty archaeologists." The scorn in her words made hot anger boil inside Betsy. She ground her teeth together to hold back words she might regret later. After all, getting angry would do her no good, and already she had told herself that she cared nothing for what the triad girls thought of her.

But she did care about what Dudley thought. She could not deny that.

Without even a good-bye, Dudley crowded into the small car and Stacy started off, jerking the car a little and making gravel spurt under its tires. None of them looked back, but Betsy saw that all of them were laughing, even Dudley. Were they laughing at her?

Before the car was out of sight Betsy bent her head and returned to her digging. She couldn't bear the sight of Dudley being taken away by those three girls who considered themselves superior to everyone else.

Only a few minutes later she had pushed all thoughts of Dudley and the triad girls into the back of her mind as more and more of the brass object emerged from the adobe dust that must have held it for many years. Although it was dulled by time and exposure to nature's whims, the gleam of old brass was unmistakable. For a time Betsy could not figure out what the object might be. When she thrust her digging spoon into the dirt in a spot that she thought must be near its edge, her spoon clinked against more of the object. Yet when she changed her digging area and moved only a little to one side, she found nothing under her spoon. What strange shape had this piece of brass taken?

At last she decided on a plan of scraping away the adobe in layers, covering a wide area to only a shallow depth. Gradually the brass object began to emerge. At first she thought it must be a ring of brass. Then she found that there was more to it as a bell shape began to emerge a little to one side of the ring. With the utmost of care Betsy scraped gently at the earth, taking great pains to control her strong urge to thrust her spoon into the adobe in a great burst of effort so that she could learn quickly the identity of the brass object.

If she scratched it she knew her mother would be disappointed, for that would reduce its value as a relic. She might even break a part of it off, for it was quite possible, she thought, that age could have made it brittle.

At last her efforts were rewarded, and she thrust her bare hands under the brass object and lifted it out. Bits of adobe clung to it, but the shape was unmistakable.

"A horn!" she cried aloud. It was made of heavy brass, more handsome than a child's toy horn. What could it have been used for? She searched through her memory for some picture that might answer this question.

The early automobiles had brass horns fastened onto

them. Could it be one of those? She thought this horn didn't quite fit that picture, but she wasn't sure. This one was twisted, bent back over itself. That was what had formed the circle she had first uncovered. It was like a long tube with the end opening out into a bell shape, and the tube twisted to form a figure like the letter *e* in handwriting. A hunting horn? Betsy wasn't sure that hunting horns had been used in this country's early days, especially not out here in the desert.

She brushed the clinging adobe from the horn and shook it in an effort to dislodge more dirt from inside the bell end. Then she clutched it carefully to her and ran to the house to show her mother the treasure she had found.

Both Mr. and Mrs. Alexander were lounging on the patio. Mr. Alexander's injured hand had kept him from his usual work around the campground, and Mrs. Alexander called out to Betsy as she came toward them, "Sorry I didn't make it to help you, Betsy. I'm feeling nice and lazy this morning."

Betsy was too excited to reply to this. She held out the horn and yelled, "Look what I found in the d—, in the ruin." She was scarcely aware that in her excitement she had almost fallen into the trap of calling it the dump the way the triad girls did.

All the laziness that Mrs. Alexander had claimed dropped away from her and she sprang to her feet and hurried to see what Betsy had brought.

Even Betsy's father showed interest in the brass horn. All of them speculated about what the horn might have been used for, but none of them could be sure.

"It's got to be pretty old," Mr. Alexander said. "The old stagecoach station's been closed for a long time."

"Maybe this will help you with your composition, Betsy," Mrs. Alexander said. "With it to go on, you may be able to find something helpful in the library."

Betsy sighed. "I'm afraid not. I looked through everything they had, but it all seemed to be dates and where the stagecoach ran, nothing about what they kept in the stations."

"Of course, the stagecoach carried mail as well as passengers," Mrs. Alexander said. "Maybe this horn was something that was being sent to someone along the route."

Betsy sank down on a lounge chair. "In that case, it could have been used for anything. It could have belonged to anyone. We may never find out what it was really used for." She set her elbow on her knee and rested her chin in her palm as she thought.

Suddenly she brightened. "I know! I'll ask Mrs. Nesbit if she knows anything about it. She's the one who told me there was a lot of history here. I'll ask her tomorrow."

Spurred on by this find and her curiosity about it, Betsy spent most of the day digging in the adobe. But her efforts were useless, for all she found were broken bits of china and pottery.

On Monday morning she went to school early so that she could stop by the office and ask Mrs. Nesbit if she knew anything that might give her a hint about the brass horn. She thought about taking the horn to show her, but decided against that. For one thing, her mother wanted to spend some time today polishing the brass to bring back something of its original shine. For another, Betsy didn't want to risk losing the horn or having anything happen to it while she attended her classes. And then, if she should find something about the horn's history, she might be able to use it in her theme for Mr. Logan. In that case, she'd want to bring the horn, restored to its lovely luster, to illustrate her theme.

Mrs. Nesbit was glad to see her. "Hello, Betsy," she said as Betsy stepped through the doorway. "Are you getting used to our desert?"

"Well, I suppose so, in a way."

"I hear you showed real presence of mind in an emergency the other day."

Betsy stared wide-eyed at her. "How did you know about Timmie?"

Mrs. Nesbit smiled. "The ranger's been singing your praises ever since. Guy and Molly Olson are old friends of my husband and me. He was really impressed by your responsible attitude."

"But it was my fault that Timmie got away."

Mrs. Nesbit's smile was gentle. "I have some children of my own. I know very well how quickly they can get into all kinds of mischief if you so much as blink your eyes. It was how you handled the situation that impressed the ranger, and everyone else."

"I'm glad, Mrs. Nesbit. But what I came to see you about this morning is a brass horn."

Mrs. Nesbit blinked her eyes in surprise, and Betsy explained about the horn she had found in the ruin that had been the old stagecoach station. "I thought since you knew that ruin had history, you might know something about this horn."

"Have you looked in the library?"

Betsy nodded. "There's nothing much there. Just dates and the route the stagecoach covered."

Mrs. Nesbit drew her brows together in a thoughtful frown. She leaned her elbow on her desk and with her index finger tapped her forehead as if that might jog her memory. At last she rose to her feet, pushing back her chair on its rollers. "I'm afraid I haven't a clue, but maybe this booklet might help you. Guy Olson gave it to me several years ago. You may borrow it if you like." She went to a low shelf of books and stooped to reach the lowest shelf.

She ran her finger along the row of books until she came to one that was held together by a row of plastic rings. She drew this one out, and Betsy saw that it was a paperback guidebook of the Anza Borrego desert. "You might just find something helpful here," she said as she handed the book to Betsy.

Betsy took the book and said, "Oh, thank you so much, Mrs. Nesbit. I'll be ever so careful with your book and return it as soon as I've finished with it."

"I know you will, Betsy. I wouldn't lend a book to just any student, but you're a responsible person."

Betsy thanked her for the compliment, but deep in her thoughts she knew she'd rather be praised for any of a number of other qualities than responsibility, like if a boy should say she was a fox, or really neat, or even beautiful. Being called responsible made her seem dull and stuffy. Nobody would think of calling Stacy Carlat responsible, but look how easily she took Dudley away from Betsy.

Much as Betsy liked Mrs. Nesbit, she thought she'd rather have praise from Dudley deShon.

Of course she had promised herself that she would not copy the triad girls, that she would be her own person. But that didn't mean she couldn't be the kind of person Dudley liked. As she left Mrs. Nesbit's office, she decided that she would have to work on being the kind of person Dudley liked without sacrificing her individuality. It was no small undertaking.

Chapter Twelve

Betsy could hardly wait for a chance to look through the booklet Mrs. Nesbit had loaned her. But she had to hurry on to her homeroom because the last bell would ring any minute.

In mid-morning she had a study hall, and she started right in as soon as she sat down, to look though the book.

She found some interesting pictures of this part of the desert, some of them taken in the present, while others showed the desert the way it was in the past. Much of the description of the Butterfield Stagecoach run had been covered by the books she had found earlier in the library. The study hall period was almost over when she came across the first really interesting accounts. She laughed to herself when she read that the first mail run to the Far West, crossing miles of Colorado desert on mule back, was called the "Jackass Mail." Later, a second and larger contract was awarded to John Butterfield, and in 1858 the first pouches of mail left St. Louis, Missouri, on the Butterfield Overland Mail, headed for San Francisco, California.

Farther on in the book, Betsy came across a bit of information that sent excitement shivering along her spine. John Butterfield's instructions to the drivers of the mail coach were, "Nothing on God's earth must stop the United States mail." In order to insure a safe and fast passage, the drivers changed horses or mules at various coach stops along the way. To save time in this process, according to the booklet, when the driver came within a mile of the station, he started blowing his horn to let the keeper of the station know he was coming. The station keeper could then get the fresh horses out of their stalls and ready them for a quick changeover.

Maybe, Betsy thought, the horn she had found was one of the horns used for this signal. She was so excited that she could hardly turn the pages of the booklet without running the danger of tearing them.

These were real people! For the first time she had seen the historical figures the way Pete saw them, as real people with real feelings and thoughts just as people had today.

Before she found any further information that would tell her if her horn might have been used on the stage run, the bell rang and she had to go on to her next class.

At lunch that day, Betsy took her usual place beside a small table, alone. Since the triad girls had given her a bad mark, none of the other girls dared to show any friendliness. Not even Pete Davis joined her today. He sometimes worked in the cafeteria. Or maybe Stacy Carlat had already grabbed him. Today Betsy didn't mind. She could hardly wait to read some more in the book Mrs. Nesbit had loaned her.

"Hi, Betsy, is this seat taken?" The voice surprised Betsy so that she couldn't believe another girl was speaking to her. But when she looked up, Lisa Abbott stood beside her, looking directly at her. She couldn't be mistaken.

"Of course not, Lisa," Betsy said. "Sit down if you want to." That didn't sound very friendly, Betsy realized, but she couldn't believe that anyone would go against the triad girls to join her.

Lisa pulled out the chair and sat down, smiling. "I've wanted to be friendly with you," she said. "But until now, well . . . you know."

Betsy knew all right. It was because of Stacy, Tina and Margo that Lisa couldn't be friendly. It had been the same with Kathy in math class. But how could Lisa be friendly now? Betsy said nothing, just tried to make her face show open friendliness and interest.

"Well, Stacy says your campground is kind of neat. She said she stopped by to see it the other day, and there were some interesting people camping there."

Betsy laughed to herself. Lisa had revealed the key to the mystery of her friendliness. Because Dudley was staying in the Sagebrush RV Park, Stacy approved of it, and that meant that she had to give a certain amount of approval for Betsy. Poor Lisa and all the other girls who were afraid to break away from the rules set by the triad girls.

"Why don't you come out to the campground and see for yourself, Lisa, instead of taking Stacy's word for it?"

"I'd love to, Betsy. Mrs. Nesbit said you have a real archaeological dig out there. It sounds fantastic. I'd like to help you hunt for relics." Her face clouded over abruptly. "I wonder if Stacy would get uptight if I just went out there myself?"

Betsy gave a small sigh of exasperation. "Lisa, you're a big girl now. It's time you stopped letting Stacy run your life."

She had spoken in a normal tone of voice, and as she finished her sentence she looked up to see Stacy herself standing beside the table. "Oh, uh, hi, Stacy," she said and hoped her face hadn't turned as red as the berries on the pepper tree at the edge of the courtyard.

"Hello, Betsy," Stacy said without either anger or enthusiasm. "Tell Dudley I want to talk to him." With a turn of her shoulder she cut Betsy off as she said to Lisa, "Come on, let's stop by the john on our way to class. We've just time to check our hair."

Lisa rose to her feet, gathered up her lunch dishes and followed Stacy. Like a sheep, Betsy thought.

With a sigh she picked up the scraps from her own lunch and carried them to the trash container. She hadn't made any progress in her friendship with Lisa, yet talking to her had kept Betsy from looking for more information in the booklet on the history of the Anza Borrego desert.

When school ended for the day, Betsy went to her locker where she picked up the books she would need to study this evening. She included Mrs. Nesbit's desert book with the others, for she intended to spend most of her study time on that one. She went outside to where she had left her bicycle in the racks. She was arranging all her books in the bike's basket when she heard someone call her name.

"Hey, Betsy!" It was Dudley's voice, and when she looked around she finally located him. He sat in the dune buggy which was parked beside the curb. "Want a ride?" he called to her.

She unlocked her bike and wheeled it across the sidewalk to talk to him. "Are you going right back to the campground?" she said. "I've something to look up for my report. I'd planned to spend—"

"Agh! Forget work," he said with scorn. "Like I told you, you take life too seriously. Come on. We're going to Julian to see what's going on there. Everybody's going to Julian these days, it must have something."

She had heard that Julian was a small town that was full of history. Maybe she would find something there to help her with her report. Besides, Stacy Carlat had irritated her during lunch period with her order to tell Dudley she wanted to talk to him, then ignoring her and taking Lisa away. Let Stacy get in touch with Dudley on her own. It was every girl for herself, the way Stacy played it, and Betsy wanted Dudley to like her. If she should turn him down now he might never ask her again. "Okay, Dudley, I'd like to go. Just let me phone my mother and tell her I'll be later than usual getting home from schoool," she said.

"Have to check in with your mom, huh? They sure keep tabs on you."

Betsy stiffened. "They care about me! My parents aren't overly strict, but all of us try to be considerate of each other."

"Well, la-de-da, the kitten shows her claws again. Sorry, sweetheart. I didn't mean to tromp on your toes. Go ahead and call Mama. I'll take that time to load your bike and books in the dune buggy. But don't waste time. I might not wait for you."

Betsy knew he meant what he said. She hurried to the pay phone reserved for students' use, made the call and explained when her mother sounded apprehensive about her going off with Dudley, "I think I can find some goodies for my report on the history of the stagecoach." That seemed to ease her mother's concern, and Betsy hung up the phone and hurried back to Dudley.

On her way she happened to glance toward the parking lot where students with cars could park. Her breath caught in her chest when she made out the two figures that could be none other than Pete Davis and Stacy Carlat, walking hand in hand toward the parking lot.

So, Betsy thought, Stacy was after Pete again. Since Dudley had come for Betsy, Stacy turned to Pete. Or was it the other way around? Maybe Dudley had asked her because Stacy was going somewhere with Pete. Well, why should she care? Dudley was more exciting than Pete anyway, and she should be glad he had asked her. But for some reason the desert sun seemed less bright, the balmy autumn air seemed to have an underlying chill that Betsy couldn't throw off.

When she joined Dudley again, however, she could almost forget about seeing Stacy and Pete together. Dudley had her things stowed in the back of the dune buggy, and he was sitting in the driver's seat revving up the motor as if to hurry her. Betsy made it a point not to change her pace. She wouldn't let him know how really eager she was to please him.

"Climb in, doll, and let's take off," he said.

Betsy barely had time to get her second leg over the side so that she could sit in the bucket seat when he started off so suddenly that she was pressed against the seat back.

The drive to Julian took them up a road that twisted around a small mountain. Dudley kept up a running patter, mostly about himself, as he drove. He was a good driver, his hands seemed relaxed yet strong on the steering wheel as he negotiated the vehicle around one curve after another. But he wasted no time slowing down for the tortuous curves. Betsy had to grip the edge of the seat to keep from being flung from side to side. If she closed her eyes she could almost believe she was riding in a roller coaster. It was a little scary but very exciting.

At last they reached the top where the road stretched out straight ahead for miles until they came to an intersection. Here they turned into a highway that was more heavily traveled.

"It looks as if everyone in Southern California is going to Julian this afternoon," Betsy said.

"Yeah, there must be something really big there."

Now as the road climbed they gradually left the desert behind. Scrubby bushes gave way to stunted trees, and with the increase in altitude the countryside began to show evidence of greater moisture. Here the trees grew taller until in an area where the road was bordered by thick woods of tall pines and other trees, some of the leaves had turned to brilliant yellow. There were even touches of red among the foliage, all mixed in with the rich green of the evergreens.

"Aren't the trees beautiful!" Betsy exclaimed. "It's so good to see trees and green things again, isn't it, Dudley?"

"Yeah, I guess," he said indifferently. "But Julian

had better produce something more than a bunch of leaves, after we've wasted all this time."

When they reached the little town, Betsy saw that cars had been parked along both sides of the main street, while people strolled the sidewalks and streamed in and out of the buildings.

"Dudley, look at that neat old building!" Betsy pointed to a Victorian structure with ornate carving decorating the narrow porch that ran the entire length of the white- and green-painted building. "Look! The sign says it's a museum. Let's go in and look around."

He pulled a long face. "Museums, yech! They're dry and dusty. They even smell stale."

Betsy laughed. She drew in a deep breath of the pine-scented air, but she could almost imagine she smelled the acrid odor of antiquity that often clung to a museum. "If all those people are going in, there must be something interesting inside."

"What I'm looking for, doll, is action. Museums are dead city."

"Well, there's a general store. That might be interesting to browse around."

Again Dudley grimaced. "Yech! And yech! I wouldn't be caught at a dogfight in any of the grungy clothes these hick towns sell."

Betsy had only to glance at his handsome fawn-colored slacks, the snakeskin belt that held them up, and his gleaming leather boots, not the same ones she had spilled whitewash on the first day he came to the campground. She knew that what he said was absolutely true.

"If this is all Julian has to offer, we're wasting our time, sweetheart," he said.

"There must be something to bring so many people here. It isn't even a weekend," Betsy said, "Let's ask."

The first available person to ask was a young man who rode up on his motorcycle and stopped in the lane beside them at a stop sign. Dudley leaned across Betsy and called out, "Hey, man, what's the main attraction here? Why's everybody gathering in Julian?"

The man on the motorcycle looked surprised. "Why, man, didn't you see? It's autumn!" His mouth spread wide in a grin. "You know, the leaves." His gloved hand left the handlebar of his bike to gesture, and his head turned as his eyes followed the gesture. He was smiling as if he had just discovered the lovely colors.

Dudley shook his head. "Crazy, that's what they are. Every one of them. Going all out over a bunch of lousy leaves. Come on, love, let's go find some action."

Without waiting for her agreement, he swung the dune buggy around in a U turn and headed back the way they had come, driving as fast as the heavy traffic and the narrow street permitted.

The roar of the motor covered the sigh that escaped from Betsy's throat. There went her chance to check on some points of history that might help her with her theme. Pete would have gone to the museum, she thought, and was suddenly shocked to find her thoughts straying to him, especially when she was with Dudley.

"Hey," Dudley said, breaking into her thoughts. "The day is still young. Let's take a run down to the border. There's more action in Mexicali than here. Even Calexico. That town on this side of the border is better than this dump."

"No, Dudley," Betsy said. "You know how my mom feels about my going down there."

"So who's to tell her? What she doesn't know won't hurt you."

Betsy set her shoulders. "Like I told you, in our family we don't lie."

"So you're going to spend your life tied to your ma's apron strings?"

"Of course not. I'm just not ready for some things yet."

"So I've noticed."

Annoyance spread heat up over Betsy's face. Why did Dudley have to make her feel so naive, so like a child? It wasn't fair. "You're on your own, but then you're older. Maybe when I'm your age I'll be on my own too," she said firmly.

He turned to give her a twisted grin. "Look, doll, I was younger than you when I just told my old man I'd had it at home. So I split."

"You just walked out? How'd you get a job at that age? I mean, a good enough job to, you know, live on your own?"

"Job? Me? You've got to be kidding! Why work when you don't have to? My grandparents left me a bundle. When that was gone I told my old man I had to have a steady flow of the green stuff. He blew his cool, but I talked him into giving me a split of deShon Plastics's profits." He turned his head to grin at her. "Smart people use their heads to keep from being tied down to the heart attack circuit."

Betsy drew her brows together. "But don't you want to do something? Don't you feel useless?"

He laughed. "Why should I feel useless, love? I'm doing something. I'm having fun. That's what life's all about."

Betsy frowned. "But I thought you said you were trying to find yourself."

"That's what I give out for publicity, sweetheart. Actually, I'm doing my own thing, the thing I'm best at. Having fun. I look for a place where I can have fun with action, and I stay there until the fun gets stale, then I move on."

It was a strange philosophy, Betsy thought, but she didn't want him to move on from here. Not yet. "You're still having fun in Shelter Valley, aren't you?" she asked.

He shrugged his shoulders. "It's getting kind of dry and dusty here." He turned to wink at her. "But I'm counting on you, love, to keep the action going."

He was the nearest to a boyfriend that she had. Besides that, he was the guy everyone wanted. As long as Betsy had Dudley, life here was bearable. If he should leave . . . She shuddered. "I'll help you find fun things to do here, Dudley."

He took one hand from the wheel and put his arm around her shoulders to draw her closer to him. "Great, sweetheart. As a team we'll turn this desert upside down. Man, we'll have big fun on the desert-o." He chanted the last words and bent his head to kiss the tip of her nose.

The dune buggy swerved on the curving road, and he had to grab the steering wheel to bring it under control again. Betsy was glad in a way to be released from his embrace because the bucket seat had not been designed to allow her to lean toward him, and its plastic hardness dug into her flesh. On the other hand, her heart sang. Dudley had hugged her and kissed her, even though the kiss touched only the tip of her nose. That must mean that he liked her and he would stay in Sagebrush RV Park for a while longer. She would have to try to think up new activities to keep him amused.

"Hey, Dudley, I know what we can do," she said. She told him about Mrs. Nesbit's booklet. "It might have something about interesting places to go in the desert. Why don't you come into my house and we'll make some lemonade and look at the book. We can plan something exciting to do."

"Lemonade? Look at a picture book? Yech! Sounds like something straight out of my great-grandmother's day. No thanks, doll. I'll pass this one up."

She had goofed again. When would she ever learn to act sophisticated?

Dudley seemed to be in a hurry now. He said little on the remainder of the drive, and when at last he swung the dune buggy into the driveway of the Sagebrush campground and stopped in front of her house, he leaped out and began to unload her bicycle from the back.

Betsy reached back to gather up her books. They were scattered over the floor as if all the swinging around the curving mountain road had sent them sliding back and forth.

One by one she picked up her books. Some of the papers she had tucked in between the pages had come out and been blown under ledges and into corners, and it took her a little time to gather all of them up. Dudley was standing with her bicycle and he appeared to be impatient, so she hurried.

When she had picked up everything in sight, she climbed out of the dune buggy, dumped her books and papers into the basket of her bike and took its handlebars from Dudley. "Thanks for the ride," she said and knew that she sounded stiff but didn't care.

"Sure, sweetheart. Anytime." To her surprise he grinned at her. "Maybe next time we'll kiss and make up, huh?"

She couldn't help laughing. After all, Dudley was Dudley. You had to take him as he was. She slanted a look up at him. "I won't promise anything, Dudley, but I'll take the matter under consideration," she kidded.

"Whoopie!" he shouted. "From you, baby, that's like a confession of love. I'll take you up on it. Really!"

She couldn't stay mad at Dudley. There was something about him that was . . . well, irresistible.

He had one foot over the side of the dune buggy when Betsy remembered Mrs. Nesbit's book. It wasn't with the rest of her books when she dumped them into the basket of her bicycle. She'd been so caught up with her thoughts of Dudley that she hadn't noticed its absence until now.

"Wait, Dudley!" she called, dropping her bike to the ground in such a hurry that it scattered her books out of the basket. She ran to grab hold of the back of his shirt.

"Hey," he said, swiveling his head around to grin at

her. "You've relented. You're going to Mexicali with me!"

"No, Dudley. It's Mrs. Nesbit's book, the one I told you about. I must have left it in the dune buggy."

He muttered something under his breath. Betsy thought they were swear words but she paid little attention and didn't care if they were or if he was angry. She couldn't lose Mrs. Nesbit's book. "Just let me crawl into the back and look once more. I'm sure it's back there under something." Without waiting for his permission she climbed into the dune buggy, crouched down to give the back a thorough going over. She found only sand and a few odd twigs from dried plants. There was no book anywhere in the dune buggy.

"You did put it back there with the rest of my books, didn't you, Dudley?"

"Love, how do I know what I dumped in there? You gave me a stack of kiddie books and I didn't see any reason to inventory them. I just dumped them back there. Come on, sweetheart, get out. I gotta split."

"But, Dudley, it was Mrs. Nesbit's book."

"So what's that to me? I don't even know the old doll. Get her another book if it's going to rock the boat."

"Don't you dare talk that way about Mrs. Nesbit!" Betsy said, but already he was revving up the motor, even making the wheels move a little, and Betsy climbed out quickly to avoid getting hurt.

She was safely on the ground when he started out, but she had to turn away from the spurt of gravel that showered her as his tires skidded along the driveway and he zoomed out into the main road and disappeared.

For a few minutes Betsy stood glaring into the distance after him. It was nothing but selfishness that made him care so little about her problems, her responsibilities. And now Mrs. Nesbit's book was lost. Every time she was with Dudley, it ended in unpleasantness or disaster of some kind.

Of course, it wasn't actually Dudley's fault that the book was lost. Betsy herself should have been more careful about how her books were stowed in the dune buggy. She'd been so excited about going off with Dudley that she hadn't thought about much else.

If she had come home instead of going to Julian with him, Mrs. Nesbit's book would never have been lost. Betsy sighed. Maybe she should just tell Dudley she didn't want anything more to do with him.

She couldn't do that. It was impossible and she knew it. Life's for fun, she told herself, quoting Dudley. She was entitled to have some fun, wasn't she?

This argument didn't do much to ease the guilt she felt over losing Mrs. Nesbit's book. With head and shoulders drooping, she walked toward the house. Never, not even since she came to the desert, had Betsy's spirits been as low as they were now.

Chapter Thirteen

Betsy felt so terrible about losing the book Mrs. Nesbit had loaned her that she couldn't bring herself to tell her parents about it. When she came into the house her mother was in the kitchen preparing a casserole for the evening meal.

"Did you have a good time with Dudley?" Mrs. Alexander asked.

"Yes, but— Oh, sure. We went to Julian. A lot of people go there to see the fall colors in the leaves."

"That must be lovely," her mother said.

"Yes, but—" Betsy broke off, then began again. "There's not much else in Julian . . . I guess."

Mrs. Alexander rinsed her hands at the sink, then as she dried them on the fluffy terry towel hanging nearby, she turned to give Betsy a direct look. "Do you really enjoy being with Dudley, Betsy?"

"Yes, but— Oh, Mom, today I'm nothing but a yes-butter. My head aches and I've got tons of homework."

"Why don't you lie down and take a little nap before supper, dear. There's time and I can get along without your help with the meal tonight. You'll be fresher later to tackle your homework."

Betsy tried for a smile. "Thanks, Mom. Sure you feel up to going it alone?"

"More able than you look, dear." Mrs. Alexander's smile was full of sympathy. "You look tired. Or troubled. Anything I can help with?"

Tears welled up in the back of Betsy's throat to all but choke her. But it wouldn't be fair to dump her own burden on her mother's shoulders when her mother was just getting back her strength. No, she'd have to learn to stand on her own feet. Dudley had been right about that, only not exactly in the way he had meant it. At least she had learned something from him.

"Thanks, but I wouldn't want to give you this headache even if I could," said Betsy. "A nap should fix me up fine." She hurried out of the room before she gave in to weakness and either blurted out her whole problem to her mother, like a little kid, or else began to blubber like an equally young one.

In her room, she couldn't sleep for worrying about the book. She'd have to replace it, but how? Since she had come to the desert she hadn't seen a single bookstore. She didn't remember the exact title of the book, let alone the author or the publisher, so she couldn't send away for it. The headache she had used as an excuse was becoming real now, throbbing away to make even thinking impossible.

She managed somehow to get through the meal without telling her parents about losing the book. But later, her evening of studying proved to be almost useless. She could not concentrate on history or math, and her Spanish textbook might as well have been written in Indian picture writing, for all she understood it.

The thought of Indian picture writing made her think of Pete Davis. Dependable was the way Mrs. Nesbit had described Pete. What would he think of her when he found out how undependable she was?

Oh, why should she care what Pete Davis thought anyway? He was probably in love with Stacy Carlat. At least, the two of them spent enough time together. On the other hand, Stacy kept running after Dudley. Why did life have to be such a muddle anyway, with everybody liking all the wrong people and wanting people to do things that were against what their families felt was right, and always getting into fights and— Betsy flung down her pencil, put her arms down on her desk and buried her face in them while she gave herself up to complete misery.

The next morning was cold, with a raw wind sweeping across the valley while clumps of heavy, gray clouds gathered in the sky. A perfect match for her mood, Betsy thought, for the cloud that had darkened her thoughts since she discovered the loss of Mrs. Nesbit's book seemed as dark as the one overhead.

"I'll drive you to school this morning, Betsy," her father offered when she came to breakfast. "It's no fit day to ride your bicycle, especially since you have to cross that dry creek bed. This is flash flood weather if I ever saw it."

Betsy had hoped that the wind might blow the cobwebs of despair out of her mind, but she had heard how suddenly a flash flood could sweep down an ordinarily dry creek bed and wipe out cars and even portions of the road itself. It was no time to be out on a bicycle.

After her father let her out at school, Betsy waited until he had driven away, then she scurried around the building and in through a side door so she wouldn't have to pass Mrs. Nesbit's office. This morning she couldn't face Mrs. Nesbit's cheerful greeting or the question she was sure to ask about whether Betsy had found anything helpful in the book.

At lunch Lisa joined her again. "I hear you went to Julian with Dudley deShon yesterday, Betsy," Lisa said.

Betsy frowned at her. "How did you know that?"

"Oh, a little bird told me," Lisa said with a smug grin.

Betsy didn't really need to ask. It had been Stacy

Carlat who told her, of course. Dudley must have gone right over to Stacy's when he left Betsy. That's what I get when I turn him down, she thought. I literally threw him into the arms of another woman.

On the whole, however, the lunchtime visit with Lisa was pleasant. For one thing, Lisa wore a purple skirt with a pale lavender top, and her blond hair was parted on the side. For once she wasn't a carbon copy of Stacy and the triad girls.

"I decided to take your advice, Betsy," she said when Betsy commented on this. "Stacy, Margo, and Tina put out the word that they were wearing knickers today, but I had this new outfit I wanted to wear, so I just reminded myself that you would do what you wanted to do without following them."

"Your outfit's really super, Lisa. And your hair's much more becoming this way."

Lisa's smile was broad. "I'm so glad you think so. It's ever so much easier to make it go this way than trying to part it in the middle the way they do."

Nevertheless, when the lunch period had ended, Lisa left Betsy and hurried to catch up with the three girls who were walking arm in arm out of the lunch area.

As Betsy watched her go, she thought, It isn't easy for people to learn to stand on their own feet. With a sigh she realized that she was struggling to do the same thing, although in a slightly different way. If she had any backbone she'd forget about Dudley deShon, let Stacy have him.

But how could she bear Stacy's smugness if she gave up? Besides, Dudley was the only boy who took her out. The Thanksgiving dance at school was coming up, and she'd counted on giving her ego a boost by showing up with Dudley. If she didn't ask him she probably wouldn't get to the dance at all. She only hoped he wouldn't think a high school dance was too juvenile for a man as old as he was. She decided she had better ask him right away before Stacy Carlat beat her to it.

During the day the weather cleared, the wind died down and the clouds disappeared, one by one, from the sky. Betsy doubted that her father would pick her up since the danger of flash floods had passed and he had so much to do in the campground. It would be a long walk home but not an impossible one. Maybe on the way she could plan how to tell her parents about losing Mrs. Nesbit's book. She needed their advice on how to try to find another one to replace that one, or what to do if she couldn't find another one.

When the bell rang for the end of the school day, Betsy hurried to her locker. She took only the books she absolutely needed to prepare the next day's assignment, leaving the others so that she wouldn't have such a load to carry. She came out the side door, again avoiding Mrs. Nesbit while at the same time hating herself for her cowardice. When she came around to the front of the school building, the sun caught a flash of red beside the curb. Her heart leaped with pleasure. It was Dudley in his red Porsche. He must have brought it back from the dune buggy rental place, and he had come to take her home in it. She waved and started to hurry across the sidewalk to join him.

She had taken only two steps when she stopped abruptly. Dudley had not returned her wave. He wasn't even looking her way, probably hadn't even seen her. But Betsy saw the person he was waiting for. She might have guessed. It was Stacy Carlat, and as she joined Dudley he took her books and tossed them into the back of the car. Just the way he had done before with Betsy's books. A lump of cotton seemed to block her throat, threatening to choke her, while she felt hot blood creep up into her face.

"Hi, Betsy." The sound of her own name made Betsy swing around. She faced Pete Davis's grinning, freckled face. "I was afraid I'd missed you."

"I came out the side door," she said, and didn't try to answer the question in his eyes. Nobody used the side door.

"You a skier? Snow skier, that is," he said.

"Not really. When we lived in Chicago I skied a couple of times on an indoor practice hill, but you couldn't call that real skiing."

"Hey, that's great! That's enough experience for dune skiing. You could phone your parents and tell them you're going out to see some Indian pictographs with me. That is, if you want to and haven't any other plans for this afternoon."

"Dune skiing?" Betsy couldn't believe that Pete had really asked her to go somewhere with him.

"You wouldn't even have to go home to change. The jeans and jogging shoes you're wearing will be fine," he said. "You'll go, won't you?" He begged her with his eyes as he asked. "If you don't have change for the phone I could let you have some."

"Thanks, I have some. But what's dune skiing? I never heard of it."

Pete laughed. "I doubt that many other people have either, but it's a great way to get across those dunes down by Glamus."

"I don't even know where that is," Betsy said.

"You don't need to know, girl. Just come with me."

Betsy was so thrilled that she wouldn't believe Pete might have intended to take Stacy but that Dudley beat him to her. Maybe Pete had been jilted just as she had, but Betsy blocked from her mind all thoughts of Dudley and Stacy too.

When she phoned home, her mother said, "That's nice, Betsy. I'm glad you're going to be with someone your own age for a change."

Betsy winced at the oblique reference to Dudley as she hung up. When she turned back to Pete, he said, "Okay?"

"Okay." She grinned. "Now tell me what dune skiing is."

Instead of explaining right then, he led her to his car parked in the students' parking lot. In a ski-carrying rack fastened to the roof of the car were two pairs of wood skis, one pair shorter than the other. "They're old and beat up," he said. "But they're great for what I want. I found them at a swap meet and bought them for peanuts. Nobody wants skis in the desert. Nobody but me, that is." He explained that the long, skinny shape identified them as cross-country skis, not downhill skis.

Betsy admitted that she didn't know much about either kind of skiing, then wished she hadn't made the admission. Pete would probably think she was dumb.

He didn't. Instead, he seemed to like explaining to her. "These aren't the plastic-bottomed skis that are popular for cross country now. They'd have to be waxed for snow use."

"But the sand would gum up in the wax," Betsy said, grinning because she knew this much at least.

Pete returned her grin. "Exactly." He told her that he had figured if skis would slide on snow, they would probably slide on loose sand like that in the dunes. "As it turned out they don't slide much, but it's more fun crossing the dunes on the boards than plowing through all that loose stuff on your feet."

Betsy watched him as he talked. There was something undeniably likable about Pete, perhaps his enthusiasm. But of course it was more of a challenge to be with Dudley.

Pete opened the car door and Betsy slid into the seat beside him. His car wasn't glamorous like Dudley's Porsche. It was an old Chevy, but he kept it shiny and clean. A small nag flashed through Betsy's thoughts, suggesting that perhaps Dudley's red Porsche, like everything about Dudley, might be glitzy, gaudy, and overdone. She pushed down the thought.

Pete swung out of the parking lot and into the street, then turned onto the highway and followed that in the opposite direction from the way Dudley had taken her to Julian. Pete didn't waste any time, Betsy noted, but the ride wasn't as exciting as the one with Dudley had been. Possibly this was because there weren't any steep hills with winding roads, but Betsy thought there was more to it than that. There was definitely a difference between their two personalities.

There was a difference in the conversation, too. Where Dudley had chatted on about himself, Pete kept asking Betsy questions. How did she like her classes, her teachers, was she growing used to living in the desert? She might not have minded if it hadn't been for her guilty conscience about having lost Mrs. Nesbit's book. Did he somehow suspect that? Was he trying to get her to confess? But he couldn't know. How could he possibly know even that Mrs. Nesbit had loaned her the book?

After a time he said, "I'm sure lucky you could go today. Beginning tomorrow I'm going to help Mrs. Nesbit in the office after school every day."

Inwardly Betsy groaned. If he didn't know already about the book, he'd probably know as soon as he started working for Mrs. Nesbit. She tried to cover her discomfort by saying, "You work in the cafeteria too. You really work a lot, don't you?"

"Yeah. Saving up for college," he said. "My folks need all the financial help they can get for that. Already they've sent two kids to college."

"You have two—brothers?"

"A sister, she's the oldest, married now, and a brother."

"That must be nice," Betsy said.

"Sometimes." Pete turned briefly to grin at her. "We used to fight a lot. We get along better now that we're older." He shifted the subject back to her again as he said, "Mrs. N. said you found something in the old ruin that might prove really interesting. She wouldn't tell me what it was, said it was your thing to handle the way you want."

"I don't mind saying. It's a brass horn. I'm trying to find out if it was used on the stagecoach."

"Hey, that's great! That ought to fit right in with your theme for Mr. Logan. You are going to do the Butterfield Stage's history, aren't you?"

"Yes." Betsy had to swallow in her effort to subdue the lump in her throat that the reminder of Mrs. Nesbit's book sent there.

"You've got it made," he said with a wide grin.

Not without that book, Betsy thought. By losing it she had handed the trophy over to Pete because now of course he would win with his report on the Indian pictographs.

Fortunately, they had reached their destination by then, and Betsy was saved from having to talk more on the painful subject.

The rolling dunes that lay on either side of the highway reminded Betsy of the dunes on Lake Michigan's shores where she had gone with her parents to the park at the southern end of the lake. But there was no lake anywhere near these dunes, only great hills of sand stretching on endlessly.

Pete parked the car and they got out. While he was taking the skis down from the rooftop carrier, he said, "We'll ski a couple of miles over that way." He gestured with his hand. "And then we'll come down into a canyon. We'll have to take off the boards there because too many rocks stick out of the canyon walls." A little farther along in the canyon, he explained, on some boulders, they would find the Indian pictographs. "They're the best ones I've found anywhere, and because they're off the beaten track, nobody knows much about them."

Beyond the parking area dune buggies and the strange-looking tricycles with huge, wide tires were running up and down the dunes like so many ants crawling over the ground.

"Where we're going is across the road," Pete said. No vehicles moved over the dunes in this area, and Betsy saw that it was posted with signs reading NO MOTORIZED VEHICLES.

"That's okay for us. We'll use muscle power," Pete said.

While he was gathering the ski poles out of the rear trunk of the car, a man drove up on one of the tricycles.

"Hey, kids, you're in the wrong country," he said. "Don't you know this is sand, not snow?" He roared with laughter as he swung his vehicle and zoomed off across the sand.

"Wise guy," Pete said and laughed. "But that's what we can expect, doing something most people think is totally loony."

Betsy laughed too. It was fun, in a way, astonishing people by preparing to use snow skis on the sand dunes.

They crossed the road where they fastened the skis onto their shoes and started down the first dune. Betsy had to set her muscles to hold her back from sliding too fast. To her surprise, she didn't slide until she pushed with her poles and, following Pete's example, made skating motions with her feet.

Going up the next dune was easy, even though the grade was steep. Her skis didn't slide back and she made speedy progress. She didn't lose her balance as she had on her attempts to snow ski. All in all, Betsy found it was fun, although it really gave her muscles a workout. She was glad when they came to the canyon Pete had told her about and sat down to rest before descending into it.

Pete unhooked a canteen from his belt and gave Betsy a drink of water that she badly needed. Then from his pocket he took two sticks of beef jerky and handed her one. They sat chewing the jerky while they rested.

When Betsy looked back the way they had come, she saw that the highway, the dune buggies and tricycles, even Pete's car, had all vanished in the distance. Here on the edge of this canyon, they seemed to be lost in a sea of sand. "How do you ever find your way around in the desert?" she asked.

Pete grinned. "I know this part of the desert almost as well as I know the part around Shelter Valley."

"I hope you know the way back to your car."

"Oh, I've got it trained. I'll just whistle and it'll come to me," he said.

"Right over the sand without getting stuck," Betsy said in mock-seriousness. Suddenly the absurdity of this idea struck her and she laughed until tears ran down her face.

"Hey, I didn't know I was all that funny." Pete pulled a red bandanna from his pocket and leaned over to dab the moisture from her face. "Actually, I carry a compass, and there are our tracks in the—" He broke off. His face was very close to hers and his eyes were wide and deep as they looked into hers. She thought he was going to kiss her. Part of her wanted him to, but at the same time she was a little afraid. How should she react? Should she respond or be submissive? Maybe she should pretend she was trying to escape his embrace.

He said, very softly, "Betsy, you're pretty. I like you with your hair all windblown and tears in your eyelashes."

"They're laughing tears," she said. "Because you made me laugh." With her sleeve she brushed away the moisture, and with nervous hands she smoothed her unruly hair. The moment of tenderness had passed, but his words had brought a warm glow to settle around her heart.

"You're wasting your time," Pete said. "The wind won't let you do much to your hair, and I'm glad." He stood up and pulled her to her feet. "Come on, lazy. We won't have time to see the pictographs and get home before dark if we sit here all day."

They stood their skis upright in the soft sand and climbed down the canyon's wall. Pete went ahead and when the footing was unsteady he reached back to help her.

At last they were on the floor of the canyon. Only a short distance ahead Pete called her attention to the flat face of a boulder set halfway up the side of the canyon. "There," he said. "It's pretty hard to get any closer, but you can see the writing well enough from here."

"I couldn't read it anyway," Betsy said. She had meant it as a joke, but when she really saw the strange figures of the Indian pictographs, she was engulfed by such a sense of awe, of looking back through the centuries, that she was sorry she had made the flippant remark.

"Pete," she said, whispering as if she might otherwise wake the ghosts of the past. "Did the Indians really make those marks? What do they mean?"

There were several circles, one on top of the other, balanced, while inside each circle was another, smaller circle. All were joined together by straight lines, and several other lines jutted or snaked out from the circles.

Pete shook his head. "The ranger doesn't know what they were meant to say, and of course I don't, but Guy's going to get an archaeologist out to look at them. Maybe he'll know."

"I think this is the most exciting thing I've ever seen," Betsy said.

"Great! I knew that sooner or later I'd get you to admit the desert's a good place to be."

"Hey! Slow down! I didn't say that!"

"But you think it, or if you don't, you will. Just leave it to old Pete Davis."

Did that mean Pete intended to see more of her? But then, wouldn't she rather go someplace really neat with Dudley deShon? Someplace where other kids from Desertview High would see them together and envy Betsy? If Dudley stayed long enough at the Sagebrush RV Park, Betsy was sure he would, one of these days, take her to some really sophisticated place. By then Betsy knew that she could persuade her parents to let her go. It all depended on persuading Dudley to stay in Shelter Valley. She had to do that. She just *had* to persuade him to stay for a long time!

Chapter Fourteen

Time was running out for Betsy. The end of October was approaching, with the composition due early in November so that Mr. Logan could grade them before the Thanksgiving break. She had searched everywhere for material on the history of the Butterfield Stagecoach, but there was nothing as interesting, as complete as what she had found in the little booklet Mrs. Nesbit had loaned her, the one lost from Dudley's dune buggy. She could not find another copy to replace that one, although she had looked in every store that sold souvenir books or even magazines.

The ranger station was her greatest hope. There was a supply of bookets for sale there, on subjects related to the desert, animals of the Anza Borrego desert, plants of the desert, minerals and rocks, everything except the Butterfield Stagecoach. Guy Olson was there when she came in with her father, and he recognized her. "Hey, here's the quick-thinking baby-sitter," he said. "No more problems, I take it?"

"No, and I was lucky to get out of that mess so easily, thanks to you. I'm so glad you found Timmie."

"Don't forget Pete Davis. He gets at least half the credit. Now, what can I do for you folks today?"

Betsy couldn't bring herself to confess about losing the book Mrs. Nesbit had loaned her. After all, Guy had given it to Mrs. Nesbit. He might get angry at her for her carelessness in losing it. "I was hoping you might have something to help me with my English theme," she said. She described the subject briefly. "I don't see any booklets on that here." She waved her hand toward the display racks. "Would there be anything somewhere else?"

Guy Olson twisted his face into a thoughtful frown. "I'm afraid you're a couple of days late. We had a booklet that went into that history pretty well, but a tourist bought the last copy just the other day."

Betsy's heart dropped down to her toes. The booklet he mentioned must be an exact duplicate of the one Mrs. Nesbit had loaned her. "Will you get in any more? Soon, that is?" she asked.

"Hard to say. I'm afraid the booklet's out of print. Maybe there'll be another edition, you know, an updated one, later, but it could be a couple of years. Sorry about that."

"So am I," Betsy said.

"But as long as you're here, why don't you look around. We're quite proud of our building here."

"It's really neat." Betsy tried to smile.

"It was carefully planned to save energy," Guy Olson said. He explained that setting the building into the rocky hillside solved the insulation problem. "And the window wall along the front, with its wide overhanging eave, lets in plenty of light yet keeps out the hot sun. We use hardly any electricity."

While Betsy strolled around the huge main room, looking at the exhibits, Mr. Alexander and the ranger, who had already developed a friendship, chatted. But the exhibits didn't interest Betsy today because she was so disappointed at being unable to find another copy of the desert book. There was nothing here that might help her with her theme.

She and her father left the ranger station. On the drive back her father broke into her gloomy thoughts when he said, "Why so silent, Betsy? Something troubling you?"

She had held back as long as she could. The burden of guilt about losing Mrs. Nesbit's book was too great for her to carry alone any longer. She needed the help of someone older, more experienced, yet someone who cared. "Oh, Daddy, I did the most awful thing!" She told him how the book must have fallen out of the dune buggy. "I've tried everywhere to find a replacement for it. The ranger station was my last hope."

Mr. Alexander was quiet for a while, thinking. "Have you told your teacher that you lost her book?"

"Oh, no!" Betsy wailed. "I can't bear to do that! She said I was a responsible person. Now I've proved I'm not."

"No, Betsy, one mistake doesn't brand you forever. Your teacher might not regard it as the disaster you do. And she'd know that at least you are honest."

"Honest but irresponsible. Besides, it was the best source of material for my theme. Now I'll probably flunk English."

"Here, here." Mr. Alexander pulled to the side of the road and put his arm around Betsy while he took his bandanna from his pocket and wiped away the tears she couldn't help shedding. "This isn't life's greatest tragedy. Give me a little time and maybe I can think of something to help."

"But my theme's due next week, Daddy."

"Then we'll both worry our heads until we lick the problem. Okay?"

Betsy turned to look at her father. The lines that had been etched there since her mother's illness shocked her. He had real problems. Compared to those, hers were minor. She tried for a smile and said, "My head's hard enough. It should handle its own problems. But if you come up with a suggestion I'll give you my best hair ribbon."

"Just what I've been needing to pin back my fair

locks," he said, falling right in with her kidding.

"Oh, Daddy, you've given me a lift, even if we never come up with a solution."

"Never say never, honey." He was no longer kidding. "That cuts off your creative thinking. In other words, think positively."

The words sounded good, Betsy thought, but the only positive action she could think of for this problem would be to go to Mrs. Nesbit and confess what she had done. Yet how could she possibly make herself do that?

For the remainder of that day and all that evening, Betsy could hardly think of anything except her conversation with her father. It had made her admit what she already knew in the back of her mind: that she should go to Mrs. Nesbit and tell her that she had lost the booklet. She should face whatever tongue-lashing Mrs. Nesbit would give her. In her heart Betsy knew that Mrs. Nesbit would not chew her out for her carelessness. That was not Mrs. Nesbit's way. She would be understanding. And that would be worse than even physical punishment. Betsy's own conscience would do the chopping.

She didn't get much studying done that evening. Fortunately she had no tests scheduled for the next day, and her grades were good enough that a poor daily assignment wouldn't hurt her too badly. But even when she went to bed that night she hadn't made any decision, and she tossed and turned for a long time before she finally fell into a troubled sleep.

Sometime in the middle of the night she awoke. Moonlight streamed in through her window and lay in a bright rectangle on the carpeted floor. Far away in the distance, the bark of coyotes began, rising to an echoing wail that reverberated from every angle of the horizon.

Betsy slid out of bed and padded in her bare feet across to the window where she sat on the floor with her arms resting on the low sill as she stared out into the enchanted night.

The desert in the moonlight really appeared to be enchanted. The distant mountains loomed like dark shadows against the moon-paled sky. On top of one of the peaks a single light blinked like a tiny diamond. The desert floor that stretched out beyond her window appeared in the moonlight as flat as a tabletop, yet Betsy knew that it was split by many canyons and dry stream beds. It was decorated with the grotesque shapes of cactus and other desert plants, yucca with its arms thrust out at odd angles, and the lacy clouds of smoke trees. She had to admit that there was a certain beauty in the strange landscape. The desert was so big, it made a mere human feel humble.

Humble and yet strong. That little light high on the mountain was evidence of modern civilization, of people. The same as the Indian pictographs were evidence that the ancient people had lived in the desert. And the adobe ruin contained evidence that the early white settlers braved the desert's dangers to live here. All those centuries; all those people.

Betsy knew suddenly that she could survive too, even her own private danger of losing Mrs. Nesbit's respect. She might have to start all over again, to earn new respect from Mrs. Nesbit, but she felt certain that the Indians had had to start all over again, more than once, probably, when the desert became too much for them. They had done it for hundreds of years, and she could do it this one time. She could tell Mrs. Nesbit about losing her book, and then start all over to earn her respect again.

With this decision made, Betsy went back to bed where she fell asleep immediately and slept through the remainder of the night without more disturbing dreams.

When morning came, she slipped from her bed and stood for a moment drawing in great breaths of the dry desert air. It was crisp but not cold, and it carried the scent of wildflowers that Betsy could not name. This morning she had regained all her old vigor and enthusiasm. There was not even a hint of dread when she thought of her coming talk with Mrs. Nesbit. She knew that once the talk was over the great weight she had been carrying would leave her.

She dressed carefully, chosing an outfit that was conservative yet becoming, a full skirt in a deep shade of rose and a shirt of pale pink that made a nice contrast with her eyes. She brushed her hair until it shone and tied it back with a rose-colored ribbon.

She didn't need a wrap this morning as she pedaled her bike because the exercise warmed her. She knew by now that as the sun rose higher the day would grow warmer so that even if she ate her lunch out in the courtyard she would be warm enough.

She had started early, hoping to see Mrs. Nesbit before classes began. That way it would be off her mind and she would be free to concentrate on schoolwork.

Mrs. Nesbit was in her office, and the door was open. She looked up and smiled when Betsy came to the doorway. For one brief moment Betsy held her breath as if letting it out might allow her courage to drain out along with her breath.

"Good morning, Betsy. How's the Butterfield Stage coming along?"

Betsy swallowed. "That's what I wanted to talk to you about, Mrs. Nesbit."

"Well, come right in. I'm always glad to talk about one of my favorite subjects to one of my favorite students. My, how pretty you look this morning. Are you hoping to capture some poor, unsuspecting boy's heart? If so, you're sure to succeed."

In a rush Betsy crossed the room and sank into the chair beside Mrs. Nesbit's desk. "Oh, Mrs. Nesbit, you won't say such nice things about me when you hear the terrible thing I've done."

"Now, Betsy, it can't be all that bad. What's troubling that pretty head of yours?"

"I've lost the book you loaned me!" Betsy blurted out. "The booklet the ranger gave you, on the Anza Borrego desert."

"That isn't a real tragedy, Betsy. They sell those books at the ranger station."

"That's just it. They used to sell them! They don't have any now!" She explained about the tourist buying the last one.

"Well, then, are you sure it's lost? Maybe it slipped under a chair's cushion, or behind a bookcase. Why don't you keep on looking for a while—"

Betsy was shaking her head vigorously and she broke in to say, "It couldn't be in the house because I didn't take it in." The part about going to Julian with Dudley deShon in the dune buggy and finding it missing when they came home was the worst part of the confession because Betsy thought that Mrs. Nesbit would have the same reservations about Dudley that her mother had.

Mrs. Nesbit made no comment on Dudley, not even when Betsy explained who he was and how she happened to know him. Instead, she said, looking directly into Betsy's eyes, "You like this Dudley deShon a lot, Betsy?"

"Uh, yes, that is—" Betsy chewed on her lower lip. "He's . . . he's so exciting."

Mrs. Nesbit nodded slowly. "Yes. An older man always seems so. And it builds up a girl's ego to be seen with someone like that."

Why did her words make her feel so uncomfortable? Mrs. Nesbit showed understanding, didn't she? Betsy had to lower her eyelids. She couldn't face Mrs. Nesbit's probing glance any longer.

But when Mrs. Nesbit spoke, it was to change the subject, away from Dudley deShon. "You know, Betsy, the worst part about the book's being lost is that your theme will suffer. I think you could have found your best material in that little booklet."

"I know," Betsy said without meeting her eyes. "I'll have to work twice as hard to get half as much information. And it won't be nearly as interesting."

Mrs. Nesbit smiled at her. "That's enough punishment for so small a misdeed. I think your own conscience feels worse about the loss than I do, to be perfectly frank."

"Oh, Mrs. Nesbit, you're the greatest!" Betsy said, and on a sudden impulse she rose and threw her arms around Mrs. Nesbit. "Thank you for not being mad at me."

As she came out of the office, she met Stacy Carlat. "Well," Stacy said, "so that's how you work it to pull down an A."

Betsy stared at her. "You mean— If you think I was trying to con Mrs. Nesbit into doing something underhanded like raising my grade when it comes through the office, you don't know her as well as I do."

Stacy's smile was a sneer. "Obviously I don't. I wouldn't think of going in there and hugging her." Stacy swung away before Betsy could recover from shock enough to reply.

When Stacy had gone, Betsy strode on to her homeroom. But as she walked, her thoughts whirled. She would show Stacy Carlat how she earned her good grades. She would make her composition so good that not even Stacy could accuse her of having to use flattery as a substitute for hard work.

She had two study halls that day, and she spent both of them working on her composition. She might not have the booklet that told about the history of the Butterfield Stage, but she had read most of that part, and she remembered it. The brass horn she had uncovered made it seem real to her, and she decided to write her theme as a story, making the characters talk and giving them problems she knew they must have had. She would use all the facts she could remember. She wouldn't put in anything that would have been impossible in the real situation, but she would bring those people to life. The brass horn had first made them seem real to her, and Pete's Indian pictographs had helped.

Then, last night when she sat by her window looking out over the desert she could imagine she saw all those people going through their trials and problems in the desert. She had felt as if she really knew them. She would put together a story that would make Mrs. Nesbit respect her again, and at the same time it would show Stacy Carlat that Betsy earned her grades. She didn't resort to dishonest means to get them.

When the bell rang at the end of that school day Betsy gathered up her books and hurried outside. There was only one thing on her mind now, her composition. She had made a good start on it during study hall, and she wanted to get the rest of her homework out of the way so that she could spend the whole evening working on the theme. The more she worked on it, the more exciting it became now, and the more real the historical figures seemed to be. She hoped her father wouldn't mind if she didn't help him this afternoon.

She was so deep in her thoughts of the stagecoach run that she didn't even see the red Porsche standing beside the curb. At first she didn't even hear Dudley calling her name. When at last the sound of his voice broke through her concentration she looked up in surprise.

"Come on. I'll give you a ride," he said.

She wheeled her bike over to his car. "Are you going right back to Sagebrush?" she asked. "I've got tons of homework."

He pulled the corners of his mouth down in a grimace. "My company's more interesting than a stack of dull schoolbooks."

Once she would have agreed with him, but now she was so excited about her story of the stagecoach that she wasn't sure. She smiled at him. "And your Porche's more fun to ride in than that dune buggy. But I do have to go right home. Really."

He raised his shoulders and lowered them in an

exaggerated shrug. "There's no arguing with a woman. Okay, get in."

"You'll take me right home?"

"If I must."

Betsy put her books in the back, carefully this time so that none of them would fall out. But she realized abruptly that there was no way to stow her bicycle in the Porsche as there had been in the dune buggy. "Oh, Dudley, my bike," she said. "I can't leave it here."

"You're not very observant, are you? I had a bike rack put on the back especially for you."

"You did!" Betsy's jaw dropped as she saw the rack. "Just for me? But it must have cost—"

He leaned over and kissed her firmly on the lips. When he released her he said, "Didn't I tell you to forget about money?"

The unexpected kiss sent Betsy's emotions into a tailspin. She heard someone giggle, and that set her face on fire. She thought she couldn't endure the embarrassment. All the kids were coming out of the school building. They would have seen him kiss her. That knowledge gave her a heady sense of excitement. Dudley hadn't minded showing his preference for her.

Yet the experience had completely disrupted Betsy's composure, and she said, "Why didn't you ask Stacy to ride with you?" She could have bitten her tongue off for betraying herself that way, but it was too late.

Again Dudley's lips curved downward. "Stacy's stale. She's too easy. But you're a challenge, sweetheart. I like sweeping you off your feet in spite of that miserable conscience of yours."

He had almost made Betsy forget her determination to work on her theme. Now that she had been reminded, she said, "You can cope with my conscience on Saturday. But tonight I've a date with those dull books. Really, Dudley, I've got to get on home."

"Okay, sweetheart. But one of these days you're going to change your mind. I'll see that you do."

For the first time since she had known Dudley, Betsy didn't want him to change her mind.

When they were settled in the red Porsche and Dudley was driving toward Sagebrush, Betsy said, "Dudley, did you make sure that desert book wasn't in the dune buggy before you turned it in?"

"What book?"

"You know. The one that got lost out of the dune buggy."

He turned to grin at her. "If it got lost out of the dune buggy, how could it be in the dune buggy when I turned it in?"

"Oh, Dudley, be serious. You know what I mean."

"To be truthful, love, I didn't remember that you lost a book. Didn't you look for it yourself?"

"Well, yes, but—"

"Then it wasn't there. There wasn't any use for me to waste my time looking for it."

What better use did he have for his time? His attitude, as if he couldn't care less, irritated Betsy, and she said very little during the remainder of the drive home. But Dudley probably did not even notice her silence, for he kept up a running flow of talk, about himself. As they turned into the driveway, Betsy leaned into the back of the Porsche and gathered up her books, making sure she had all of them this time. As soon as he stopped, she slid out of the car.

Dudley sat in the driver's seat while Betsy took her bike from the rack and set it upright, bracing it with the kickstand while she picked up her books and put them in the bike's basket. He might at least have helped her unload the bike, she thought, fuming inwardly.

As soon as she had her things together Dudley took off with a spurt of gravel and a roar of the motor. He shouted back over his shoulder, "See you!"

Betsy wasn't even sure she wanted to see him. She marched toward the house, thinking that Dudley was just about the most selfish person she knew. So different from Pete Davis. She caught herself up at that thought. How had Pete happened to come into her thoughts? She didn't want to think about Pete. Not now. She turned her thoughts to her theme. She owed it to Mrs. Nesbit to make this theme good. Even more than that, Betsy had become so engrossed in the affairs of the people who had been associated with the Butterfield Stage that she had to follow them through to the end of her story.

Chapter Fifteen

The next day at lunch Lisa joined Betsy. Again she showed her own personality in her clothing and hair style, rather than that of the triad girls. And today she looked radiant.

"Betsy, I'm so happy, and it's all thanks to you," she said as soon as she sat down.

"Hey, I didn't know I was that great. How come all the good thoughts of me?"

"Harley Kellog noticed me. He told me he likes girls he can pick out of a lineup, girls who don't all look alike. See, Betsy, if you hadn't been after me to stand on my own feet, I might never have had a date for the Thanksgiving dance."

"What's the Thanksgiving dance got to do with it?"

Lisa leaned toward her across the table and said, her voice softened by awe, "Harley asked me to go with him. To the Thanksgiving dance, just about the most important bash in the whole year. That's what."

Betsy made her mouth form an O. "Lisa, that's great! I'm happy for you."

Lisa turned sober. "Betsy, you're going to the dance, aren't you?"

Betsy raised her shoulders and let them sag. "I guess not. Nobody's asked me."

"Well, dummy," Lisa chided. "Don't let that stop you. Get busy and ask somebody. How about that fox in the red Porsche I've seen you with. Why don't you ask him?"

Betsy broke off a piece of crust from her sandwich and crumbled it in her fingers, studying the procedure as she spoke, "Oh, I don't know. He's probably already tied up with Stacy Carlat."

"You don't *know* that! Ask him and see. He can't do any more than say no."

Betsy sighed. "I guess." To her own surprise she discovered that she didn't really want to ask Dudley deShon to the Thanksgiving dance.

Maybe Lisa suspected this too, for she said, "Or, if you don't want to ask him, how about asking Pete Davis?"

"Pete wouldn't want to go with me."

"I wouldn't be too sure about that."

Betsy raised her head and met Lisa's eyes squarely. "If he did, why hasn't he asked me already? The dance isn't far off and everybody's getting paired off."

"Maybe because of the guy in the Porsche. Half the school saw him kiss you the other day when he came for you."

Betsy felt the heat rise into her face. "Oh, that's just Dudley's way. It didn't mean a thing to him."

"How'd we know that? There weren't any captions under the picture to tell us."

"Well, it was only a dumb little peck, not a real kiss."

"I don't care what it was; the point is, Betsy, you've got to do the asking. The Porsche guy doesn't go to Desertview High, so he can't do the asking, and Pete thinks you're tied up with foxy Porsche. You've got to take the initiative, ask *somebody!*"

"Then I guess I won't go."

"That's dumb. You're going to sit back and let Stacy Carlat take her pick? You gave me some good advice, and I took it. Look where it landed me. Now I'm trying to return the favor."

Betsy smiled at her friend. "I appreciate it, Lisa. And I'll think about what you've said."

"You'd better think hard. And fast too."

Betsy supposed she should think about Lisa's advice, but how could she follow it? She doubted that Dudley would want to come to the dance if she asked him, and she doubted even that she wanted to take him. On the other hand, Pete cared more for Stacy than he did for her, and since he had seen Dudley kiss her Betsy knew she would be too embarrassed to ask him to take her to the dance.

During the following days she had little time to think about the Thanksgiving dance. She spent every spare minute working on her composition. No matter how many books she dug through, she found nothing that brought the people to life the way Mrs. Nesbit's book had, so she sifted through her memory for every scrap of information from it.

She was sorry she couldn't help her mother go through the ruin, although her mother seemed happy to spend a good part of each day alone at the site of the old stagecoach station, sifting through the crumbled adobe. Mrs. Alexander had found a bag of marbles that, when cleaned up, sparkled like new and showed more beautiful craftwork than the glass balls that came off today's assembly lines. She also found a metal box that contained several elaborate paper lace valentines with quaint, old-fashioned pictures and verses that were amusing in their Victorian sentimentalism.

Betsy was as excited over these as her mother was. In fact, the valentines helped her see a new character to use in her historical story of the stagecoach. Betsy saw this character as a young girl who had come west to marry the man she loved. In the story, the girl had saved all the love messages her young man had sent and she brought them with her on the stagecoach. Then, in the excitement of seeing him again, she rushed off, leaving the box of valentines to molder in the old stagecoach station.

"Oh, Mom," Betsy cried. "Isn't it the most romantic thing you ever saw, the box of valentines!"

They were old, faded, dry and brittle, in reality, but to both Betsy and her mother they were still beautiful.

While they were going through the valentines, Dudley stopped by the house. Betsy was so caught up in the excitement of the find that she thrust out the one in her hand before he had time to say more than "hi." "Isn't it lovely, Dudley? And here's a whole box of them."

The way his expression turned sour as he looked down at the faded finery she held told her how weak his enthusiasm was. "Well, I guess if that's what turns you on, but they look kind of tired," he said. "Hey, man, I've got something crisper than that. They're making a movie down in Mexicali. We can run down and catch some of the action." He turned to Mrs. Alexander. "It's an American company making the film. You'd let her go down for that, wouldn't you?" His grin was persuasive. "deShon Plastics can get us passes—"

Betsy didn't even wait for her mother to reply. Breaking in, she said, "Thanks just the same, Dudley, but these valentines have filled my head with so many ideas it'll burst if I don't go right to my room and work on my story."

He stared at her as if he couldn't believe what he had heard. "You'd take a box of scrap paper instead of a chance to catch a movie in the making?"

Betsy clutched the metal box to her. "This isn't full of scrap paper. It's full of memories of the lives of real people."

Dudley shook his head in disbelief. "Mrs. A., I'd say your daughter's got a bad case of desert fever."

Betsy's mother only smiled.

"Some other time, okay, Dudley?" Betsy said. But she knew suddenly that she was saying the words only to be polite. She didn't care if there never was another time.

When he had left, she went to her room, thinking about what he had said. Had she really caught desert fever? Had she really begun to appreciate the desert? Did that mean that she might even one day feel at home in Shelter Valley?

She wasn't ready to answer those questions yet, and she had no difficulty turning her attention to her report. Now the people who had traveled on the Butterfield Stagecoach, and the people who had run it, had come to life. She felt that she knew every one of them.

She finished her theme just in time to hand it in on the day it was due. Until then she had been certain it was good. In fact, she had been so interested in writing it that she didn't stop to consider whether it was good or poor. She was thoroughly caught up in the story she was telling about the old stagecoach run, told through the people who drove it or traveled in its coaches. She could feel the jolting of the coach as it bumped along the rutted road. She could smell the horses and see in her imagination the lather that foamed their flanks when they had been pushing hard toward the next stop where they would be replaced and could rest. Her own muscles ached from helping to push the coach up the steep Foot and Walker Pass.

But once the composition was completed and had been handed to Mr. Logan, doubts began to swarm over Betsy until her stomach churned and shivers ran along her spine whenever she thought about Mr. Logan reading— and judging—her theme. Maybe he would think it was dumb, silly, weird. In her thoughts she heard Mr. Logan say, "Betsy, your imagination is out of this world, literally. Who would believe a crazy thing like this?"

She spent a miserable weekend when she knew he would be grading the reports. She couldn't keep her mind on anything for more than two seconds, and if anyone opposed her, she burst into tears.

When Monday morning came, her father said, "I hope that teacher has graded the themes by now. Once you know the results, maybe we'll have our daughter back again."

Betsy felt a moment of contrition. "Have I really been that bad, Daddy?" she asked.

He smiled. "Well, you still look like our Betsy. But some of your actions have made me wonder if you really are Betsy." He came over and hugged her. "All kidding aside, honey, I'd be willing to give you odds that your theme is a good one. I'm no judge of high school homework, but I know how hard you've worked."

Betsy sighed. "I wish you were my English teacher." They both laughed and Betsy hurried away to school.

She pedaled her bike vigorously that morning on her way to school. She hoped the exercise would help her relax and take away the tension.

When she came into the school building, she would have passed Mrs. Nesbit's door with only a wave, but Mrs. Nesbit hailed her. "It wasn't so hard to write about history, was it?"

"Well, maybe, but I'm sweating out the results now."

Mrs. Nesbit grinned. "As you kids say, 'Hang in there.'" She waved Betsy on and bent over her own work again.

As Betsy went on, she frowned. Did Mrs. Nesbit's words of advice have special meaning? She was one of the judges. She must know the results. Did her advice to keep her spirits up mean that Mrs. Nesbit knew that Betsy was receiving a poor grade on her composition?

Cool it, Betsy, she told herself. There was no use in worrying herself sick. She couldn't do anything about it now. She'd have to stand or fall on what she had already done.

When at last Mr. Logan's English class time came around Betsy's feet seemed to drag as she made her way to the room. But eventually she arrived, and she had to go in and take her place. The triad girls were in this class too, and so was Lisa, and even Pete Davis. Everyone was here to be witness to her disgrace if Mr.

Logan thought her story was overdone. If he thinks it's glitzy, she thought, I'll simply die. Really! She hoped her face didn't show what she was thinking.

When Mr. Logan came into the room, he carried a sheaf of papers with him. Betsy thought the groan that came involuntarily from her throat sounded terribly loud until she realized that most of the others in the room had made similar sounds.

Mr. Logan grinned at them. "Hey, your themes weren't all that bad," he said. "In fact, some of them were great."

There was a general shuffling of feet in the room, and Mr. Logan made a show of arranging the papers on his desk. Obviously he was enjoying keeping them in suspense.

At last he said, "I promised you I'd award a trophy to the theme I consider the best, and I've chosen that theme."

Betsy could feel the increase of tension in the room. Her own grew with it.

"I also promised you," Mr. Logan went on, "that I would read aloud the three top ones, and I will do that." It seemed that he took forever shuffling through the papers until he finally came up with the ones he wanted. More suspense.

"First comes the composition that earned third place," he said. "It is good, very good. If it hadn't had such stiff competition, it might have earned a higher place." He began to read an article about the fossils that could be found in the Anza Borrego desert.

As Betsy listened, she almost forgot her nervousness. She was startled to learn that much of this area had, millions of years ago, been under water. Many of the fossils that had been found here, according to this article, had once been sea creatures.

When he had finished, he announced the author of report. To Betsy's astonishment, it was Tina Hatfield, one of the triad girls. How little she knew of those three girls. Maybe they had sensed her determination not to like the desert. Maybe that helped to explain their hostility. If someone had come to her school in Chicago and made no effort to hide her dislike of the area, Betsy would not have been very friendly either.

She would try from now on to be more friendly.

Her attention was caught again as Mr. Logan announced the second place report and began to read it. From the first sentence there was no doubt that the author of that report was Pete Davis. As Mr. Logan read about pictographs and petroglyphs, Betsy remembered the fun she and Pete had had that day when he took her dune skiing to see some pictographs. It gave her a good feeling to know already that pictographs were painted on the rock face while petroglyphs had been made by carving out the lines in the so-called desert rust, the discoloration made on the rocks by time and weather.

Pete's report was good. The whole class showed interest, and when Mr. Logan had finished reading it, he said, "I think this report is the nearest to what I asked for. It is well structured and informative, accurate without becoming so bogged down in facts that it's dull. This is an outstanding composition."

Betsy was so pleased for Pete that she began to clap. Others were voicing their congratulations, but no one else clapped, and Betsy stopped, embarrassed for showing so much enthusiasm. She glanced at Pete to see if he disapproved. He might think she was running after him. But Pete's head was bent and his eyelids hid his eyes, although he was grinning. His face had turned scarlet. Betsy hoped it was Mr. Logan's praise that embarrassed him, and that in the general murmur of congratulations from the class her own clapping had gone unnoticed.

Then Mr. Logan said, "Perhaps this report should have won the trophy. I debated long and hard about the decision. Your reactions to the next one, class, will show me whether or not I made the correct choice. He bent his head over the papers and began to read.

Instantly Betsy wished the floor would open up and

she could disappear into the gap. It was her theme he was reading now, and she longed to rush up and grab it away from him. Now it sounded really glitzy, overdone, gaudy, as silly as those fancy paper lace valentines. Why had she ever had such a dumb idea as writing it like a story? Mr. Logan must think she was a nerd, a total jerk. Any minute now the class would burst into laughter because they would agree with him. They'd yell, "Throw it in the dump along with the dumb box of valentines!"

But they didn't yell. They didn't laugh, and gradually Betsy began to realize that everyone's attention was focused on what Mr. Logan was reading. They were all listening as they had never listened to him before. Could it be—

Before Betsy knew it, she too had been transported by her own words back into the earlier century. Once again she was riding the stagecoach, being jostled and swayed from side to side as the top-heavy coach careened along the rutted road. She could feel the cold metal of the box that held her precious valentines. For the moment she was the young girl racing across the desert to marry the man she loved.

When Mr. Logan finished the last page, there was complete silence in the room. Then someone sighed, and a voice behind Betsy asked, "Mr. Logan, who wrote that?"

The bubble of enchantment that had surrounded Betsy collapsed suddenly, and once more she longed to sink into oblivion. Pete Davis must know that she had written the story. Was he laughing now? Would he speak up and tell the class? She didn't dare look at him. Instead, she stared down at her hands clutching each other in damp despair in her lap.

"Before I reveal the author, tell me what you thought of the composition," Mr. Logan said.

"Where can we buy the book?" someone asked.

Mr. Logan chuckled. "Exactly. It reads just like a story, doesn't it? I could tell by your faces as I read that this author has done more to turn you on to the history of this area than I could in a whole year of teaching. There's real imagination here, all based on facts. The author has captured the real feeling of the desert and of the people of that time. Do you agree with me, class, that this theme deserves the trophy?"

The chorus of "Yes!" was loud and enthusiastic.

"Betsy," Mr. Logan went on. "If you don't become a writer of historical fiction, I'll be disappointed in my ability to judge talent."

Without knowing she was going to speak, Betsy said, "But it wasn't fiction, Mr. Logan. Those were real people!" Still, he had given her an idea of how to use her baby-sitting money. She would save it to help with college. Now she had a purpose. Now she wanted to continue her education.

"The first place in the contest goes to Betsy Alexander who was a newcomer only a short time ago. I think she belongs to the desert now. She's one of us," Mr. Logan said.

It wasn't until Lisa, sitting behind Betsy, tapped her on the shoulder and said, "Go up and get your trophy, dummy," that Betsy became aware that Mr. Logan was holding out a small but very shiny silver cup. She stood up on trembling legs and made her way to the front of the room.

The bell rang to change classes, and suddenly Betsy was surrounded by members of her class congratulating her and talking about her story. Only Stacy Carlat hurried out of the room without speaking to her.

For once Tina and Margo did not follow Stacy. They came up to speak to Betsy, and Tina said, "Do you mind if we come out to the campground sometime and help you go through the adobe ruin?"

Before Betsy answered her question, she took time to congratulate Tina on her own report. "It was really fantastic, Tina," she said. "It blows my mind to think that this was all under water once. Really. It must be exciting to find those fossils in the rocks and sand."

NEVER SAY NEVER

Tina grinned. "Like digging through the adobe ruin. We're both digging for treasure, aren't we?"

Betsy agreed and told her she would be welcome at the dig any time. "Maybe you'll let me help you with yours too."

Tina nodded and then other students came to ask questions and talk about her story. A crowd surrounded Pete too. Betsy had hoped he would come to speak to her. Was he disappointed because his article didn't win first place? Perhaps she should go tell him how she had enjoyed his theme. But maybe that would seem like talking down to him. By now she had let too much time pass. Her next class was phys ed, and she would have to hurry to the gym to change and be on time. There wasn't time left to speak to Pete.

Part of her excitement of winning the trophy had been dimmed because she didn't know how Pete felt about her winning over him. And there was Mrs. Nesbit's book. Maybe she should give Mrs. Nesbit the trophy in lieu of the book she had lost.

Chapter Sixteen

Only two weeks remained until the Thanksgiving dance, and still Betsy had not been asked for a date. Neither had she found the courage to ask anyone as Lisa kept telling her she would have to do.

Winning the trophy for her composition in Mr. Logan's class brought her more attention than she had expected. Now as she walked from class to class, almost everyone, boys and girls alike, waved or called out a greeting to her. She never had to eat lunch alone now, for different groups welcomed her. Betsy made a point of dividing her time between groups so that she would not be branded as part of a single one. At home, when she worked in the adobe ruin, she often had company other than her mother. In short, Betsy felt that she belonged here now. But apparently nothing she did could convince the boys, including Pete Davis, that she wasn't Dudley deShon's girl. Pete had congratulated her on her story, had been really pleased that she could see the desert in that light now. But he didn't ask her for a date.

Betsy had given much thought to offering her trophy to Mrs. Nesbit since she couldn't return her book, but as yet she had done nothing toward that. The trophy meant a lot to her. It would be hard to give it up. More than that, she wasn't sure it was the right thing to do.

No trophy could replace the book, and it wouldn't ease her conscience. Not really.

One afternoon when Dudley came to pick Betsy up after school she gave a small sigh of regret. The afternoon sunlight gleamed on his red Porsche, although there was a crispness in the air that brought a hint of autumn even to this desert area. It would have been a perfect afternoon for a brisk bike ride home, and she would have enjoyed working in the warm sunlight with her mother on the adobe ruin. Who knew what treasure they might find on such a beautiful day?

Dudley called to her without leaving his Porsche. "Hang up your bike and I'll give you a ride home with me."

For an instant Betsy looked at him, tempted to refuse his command. That was typical of Dudley, egotistical as always, assuming that she wanted nothing more than to be with him. She had been impressed with his years, his obvious wealth, his ease in talking to people, especially her.

But now— She smiled wryly. Now she felt less enthusiastic about him. But it wasn't Dudley's fault, of course. He hadn't changed; she had. She wheeled her bike over and settled it in the rack he had installed on the Porsche, then slid into the seat beside him.

She'd let him drive her home this time. No use making a big thing of it. But she had no doubt that it would be someone other than Dudley deShon whom she would ask to the Thanksgiving dance. She really didn't care all that much about being with him. Or even about being seen with him. That, perhaps, severed the last hold Stacy Carlat had over her.

As Dudley drove along the road, the wind caught Betsy's hair and flung it back from her face and her head. It felt good, driving away the last of her doubts about herself.

Dudley didn't turn into the driveway of the Sagebrush campground. Instead, he passed the gate and went on.

"Hey!" Betsy cried. "I thought you said you were taking me home!"

"I will. In time. But first I've a surprise for you. I want to tell you about it."

"Surprise?"

"Yeah. I wanted to tell you in time so you could plan. I know girls like to get ready, maybe buy a new dress or have their hair done or something."

Betsy drew in her breath and held it. What was he talking about? Surely he wouldn't have the nerve to ask her to let him take her to her own school's Thanksgiving dance! Surely even Dudley would know that an outsider shouldn't take the initiative. "What is this surprise?" she asked.

"Are you ready for this? There's a new club opening in San Diego. It's already the talk of the whole county. All booked up on the first night. So—" He drew it out as if to impress her. "What does sharp old Dudley do? He wields the deShon Plastics's influence and wrangles a couple of tickets. I'm taking you, sweetheart!" The last sentence was spoken as if it were a priceless gift he handed her.

Betsy didn't listen to the note of promise in his voice. "When is this, Dudley?" she asked.

"Just in time for Thanksgiving. The day before, in fact. That Wednesday night. My Thanksgiving present to you."

The night of the Thanksgiving dance! "I'm sorry, Dudley. I can't go."

"Hey, now. Your mom can't object to that. San Diego's not across the border."

"It isn't my mom, Dudley. It's that that's the night of Desertview High's Thanksgiving dance."

He turned to stare at her. "You'd turn down a chance like this! For a kid's dance! You've got to be kidding!"

Betsy smiled. "I'm not kidding, Dudley. And it may be a kid's dance, but don't forget, I'm a kid compared to you." She turned serious and laid her hand on his arm. "I'm sorry to disappoint you, Dudley. Really. But I'm just not ready for a date with an older man to the opening of a sophisticated nightclub. Of course I thank you for asking me."

He looked bewildered, as if he couldn't believe that anyone would turn down such an invitation. "What'll I do? I've got the tickets, and I want to go. But it's no fun going alone."

"You can find somebody, an older girl, who'd love to go. There must be lots of girls in San Diego who'd jump at the chance."

"Yeah. Man. Lots of girls." Dudley's eyes turned crafty. "Lots of boats too." Abruptly he slowed just enough so that he could swing the Porsche around in a U turn and head back toward Sagebrush. "Lots of action too. I'll drop you off and head right down to La Jolla, that's the best part of San Diego in my book."

The strange part of it was that Betsy didn't feel sad about his leaving, while only a short time ago she had thought going to a nightclub with Dudley would be the best thing ever.

By the time he had let her out, Betsy knew exactly what she would do. She would ask Pete Davis to take her to the Thanksgiving dance. He couldn't do anything worse than say no, and he might, he just might say yes. As she hurried toward her house and the phone, her heart sang.

She didn't make it to the phone, or even to the house, for Mr. Caldwell, carrying Timmie, was walking along the drive and he hailed her "I'm glad you're home, Betsy, because we're ready to leave, and Timmie wanted to tell you good-bye."

"Timmie, I'm going to miss you," she said. "I hope you'll bring your parents and your brothers and sister back soon. Will you?"

Timmie nodded, and Mr. Caldwell said, "Also, I thought you might have more use for this booklet than I will back in the city. I want you to have it. Your dad said you were looking for material on the Anza Borrego desert." He held out a thin paperback book.

Betsy stared at it openmouthed. It was the desert booklet, exactly like the one Mrs. Nesbit had loaned her.

"I bought it at the ranger station, and I've enjoyed it while we were here. It has helped us find a lot of interesting spots. It may help you."

"Oh, Mr. Caldwell, you don't know how much this will help me! I can't thank you enough." She told him about Mrs. Nesbit's book and her English composition.

"Well, Betsy," he said. "I'll expect to see your name on a lot of books in the future."

"Thanks, Mr. Caldwell, and I hope you do."

Timmie gave her a hug and kiss, and she told him good-bye.

When they had left Betsy started on toward the house. As she walked, she stared down at the booklet in her hand. She could hardly believe that she actually had another copy of the Anza Borrego booklet. Now she could return this book to Mrs. Nesbit and her conscience would be free again. She smiled to herself. Mr. Caldwell had been the tourist who bought the last copy at the ranger station. There had been another copy of the booklet right in her own campground all along, if she had only known. She thought back to the day the Caldwells arrived to stay in the campground. How little she had suspected then what an important role that family would play in her life.

Musing on the events that had tied her in with the Caldwells, she was surprised to glance up and see Pete Davis's Chevy heading toward her along the driveway.

"Hi, Betsy," he said when he came alongside her. "I've been chasing you all day but I couldn't catch you."

"Oh?" Betsy grinned. "I didn't know I was that hard to get."

Pete didn't seem to think that was funny. "Yeah, first there was a gang around you so I couldn't get to you at school. Then after school, when you got into that Porsche, Lisa Abbott really dug into me. She said if I didn't get in my car and go after you I wasn't the man she thought I was. And—well, uh, here I am."

"I'm glad you came, Pete."

"I was afraid you'd go on somewhere with that plastic guy."

Betsy grinned. Plastic was a good word for Dudley. "Poor Dudley," she said. "He has about as much direction as the windblown sand on the desert. He's coasting along on his father's money and influence. I've just learned how important it is to stand on your own feet."

"You're not all sewed up with that guy?"

"No way. In fact, he's gone on to San Diego. I hope he'll come back for his motor home, but that's all. At least now you won't have competition from him when you date Stacy."

Pete drew his brows into a frown. "Stacy? Why would I want to go with her?"

"Well—" Who could figure men out? Betsy watched her foot draw circles in the sandy soil. "Well, I thought you did."

"You thought wrong. Stacy's always asking me to take her some place, but since you came here— Well—"

He seemed unable to go on, but he'd said enough. A wide grin spread upon Betsy's mouth as she looked up at him. "Pete, I wanted to ask—"

At the same time Pete was saying, "I wanted to ask—"

They both broke off, laughing self-consciously.

Betsy was the first to end the moment of silence that held them. "What did you want to ask, Pete?"

His face flushed and the freckles seemed to move across his cheekbones. "Will you go to the Thanksgiving dance with me, Betsy?"

"Oh, Pete!" she cried. "I was going to ask you the same thing. I'd love to go with you!"

"Really?" His voice did strange things on the scale. As if he couldn't trust it to express his feelings, he caught her to him and kissed her firmly on the lips.

The kiss didn't last very long, and when it was over they stood looking at each other, startled, as if their own feelings had surprised them and they didn't know what to do next.

"How about some lemonade?" Mrs. Alexander called from the patio. That broke the tension.

"Great!" Pete said.

"Wonderful," Betsy added. The lilt in her voice told that she meant more than the lemonade.

Pete caught her hand and together they hurried across the sandy soil to the patio.